# Rose Moon

# &

# Death on the Toilet

Fiction by Robert Stikmanz

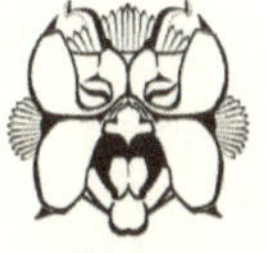

Stikmantica
Austin, Texas

Stikmantica—Austin, TX
Words, Images & Other Artifacts
*stikmantica.com*





*Rose Moon* publication history: A early version of part I appeared in *The Scroll volume 1*, Zarathustra Publishing, Tijeras, New Mexico, 2011. The novella was originally published as an ebook through Smashwords by The Blue Moose Press, Glenhaven, California, from October through December 2014. A second edition, from Stikmantica, was released through Smashwords in January 2015. This print edition was released September 2015.

"Death on the Toilet" publication history: An early version of this story was published in *The Sorcerer's Scrolls #47*, Zarathustra Publishing, Tijeras, New Mexico, October 2010. The story was published by the author as an ebook released through Smashwords in October 2011.

Stikmanz, Robert Rose Moon & Death on the Toilet /
Robert Stikmanz
p.cm. ISBN: 978-0-9838137-4-3
      1. Fiction— Literary—Slipstream—Erotica.
      2. Fiction— Literary—Speculative—Erotica.
      3. Fiction— Literary—Weird.
      4. Stikmanz, Robert

I. Title

# Acknowledgments

*Rose Moon* began as a treatment written at the suggestion of Duane Humeyestewa, with an eye toward developing a screenplay. Instead, when Jeremiah Griffin of Zarathustra Publishing invited me to write serial fiction for a new magazine, *The Scroll*, I revised and expanded the treatment into a four-part novella. An early version of part one appeared in *The Scroll #1*, the only issue produced. Set adrift by circumstances, *Rose Moon* suffered what fiction always suffers at my hands—multiple, extensive rewrites with sometimes unexpected results. Along the way the work benefited from comment by Gary Warner Kent and M. S. Lewis, and unflagging support from Paul Elard Cooley. Their gifts of time and insight were invaluable.

"Death on the Toilet" also first saw light via Zarathustra Publishing, but in a different magazine, *The Sorcerer's Scrolls #47*. Accepting the story, Jeremiah Griffin described it as "strangely heartwarming." I released it as a free ebook through Smashwords from 2011 to 2016.

This one is for my dad.

# Contents


Rose Moon

I .......................................................................... 9

II ......................................................................... 29

III ........................................................................ 55

IV ........................................................................ 89

Death on the Toilet ............................................ 115

# Rose Moon

I

A hair-thin spiral of gleaming metal shaved the end of a universal joint to its necessary tolerance. Bigger MacGregor found it satisfying in a physical way to watch precision emerge behind an unbroken, razor-edged curl. As the twist of scrap dropped away, Bigger switched off the lathe, released the shaft head and raised it to contemplate his work. Unconsciously, he hummed a descending scale, harmonizing with slowing tones of damping rotors.

When the harmonics wobbled unexpectedly, he thought first that something had gone wrong with the generator. Stripping off his face shield, he cocked an ear. The odd rumble came not from slowing machinery, but from outside. He placed the shaft head carefully beside its companion pieces on the workbench and headed to the yard for a view of the skies. His face shield landed on a tool cabinet along the way.

The morning had been still, with high-flying puffs of cloud that changed shape faster than they crawled toward the horizon. Variable winds drove through the afternoon, gusting from a weather system in the region. Bigger halted under the eave of the fabrication bay to take in the hills separating the rural world of MacGregor Pedal Cars from town. Scattered storm cells had moved close while he worked through the heat-charged afternoon. Atop trailing purple curtains of rain, the cells strode the land, twenty, thirty, sometimes forty miles apart. The fat, blue-and-white cauliflower shapes of their waists billowed upward into huge, flat-topped masses of cloud. Lightning, bright enough to smite the eyes, ranged up and down distant, blue-black squalls.

A new rumble, twin to the one that had called him out, erupted from the southwest, still miles away, beyond the shop building. His dogs lifted their heads to watch him stride into the yard to investigate, but they made no move to follow.

Angry purple boiled in the sky over Standing Rock, the hill rising from Bigger's few acres. Rapid flashes lit the gloom, but no bolts were visible above the ridge. These would not be long in coming, he was sure. A new wave of thunder cracked before it rolled.

The hair on his nape and the smell of the wind told him everything critical about changing conditions, but he checked his weather station anyway. Atop the mast bolted to an awning post on the shop, the vane whipped, now bold, now hesitant, from point to point. Perched below it, the anemometer spun and lagged without pattern. When he tapped the barometer, the needle sank. Bigger turned to his inventory.

***

MacGregor Pedal Cars—of which Bigger was owner, designer, fabricator and sales force—had twelve vehicles in the yard. Post-petroleum economics had created a market for comfortable, efficient, people-powered transport. A few corporations dominated the industry, as one would expect, but movement of goods became increasingly complex after the collapse of the old United States. This, combined with the low-tech basis of pedal car production, had inspired a thriving niche of local manufactories.

The home shops, generally, became watch words for excellence, and a few earned outsized names. The best took on an aura of cool. Shapely Frakt, legendary jam band from the Los Angeles Free State, featured their customized, nine-person MacGregor tour bus in a video. "Fang," the signature smuggler's trike of the *Howling Maze* properties, was also prominently his. The buzz was not all style. Bigger's machines were brilliant, innovative and meticulously built. It was a reputation that made possible a location far enough from town and highway that he dealt largely with people who intended to see him. Days might pass without interruption.

***

Using a hoist to stand them on end for storage, he could get four cars into the fabrication bay, but only three in the repair bay. The spaces were about the same, but as sure as he completely filled both, some contingency would raise its head and he would be sorry. Fortunately, the mix on his lot included five utilitarian models that would fare well staked under heavy tarps.

It took only minutes to wheel seven vehicles under cover and crank them into position. As befit a land with changeable weather, stakes to tie down the remaining cars were set permanently in the ground. Covering the vehicles left in the yard, he noted that the cells in the heavens clustered more densely. Brilliant daylight still reached fat fingers through the vanguard of a broader front, but the sun itself was obscured. To the west, no gaps remained in the furious sky.

Details—a tree, the ruin of a cowshed, the wind-whipped grass of MacGregor's field—shone eerily, saturated with color stark against the lightning-struck purple of the coming storm. As he moved from one car to the next, first anchoring the vehicle, then fitting it beneath a tarp, he watched the light change, shifting through a riot of hues and intensities.

He was attending the last of the vehicles, a rally version of a farm trike, when a faint shadow fell across the knot he tied. Bigger snugged the rope, noting the arrival of a visitor without looking up. He cinched a tarp over the three-wheeler as the light turned rose and golden.

The silence of his dogs surprised him. Belle's head was up, her pose inflected by coyote trace mingled somewhere in her predominantly hound ancestry. Her soft "woof" in response to his unspoken query was both assurance of no danger and a prod to step out of his thoughts. It was a sound she made for nonthreatening strangers. Usually, it meant "customer." Bigger could not imagine who would come from town to look at pedal cars with dark close and heavy weather on the way.

Toro, an oversized male version of Belle, exhaled noisily. The signal was unambiguous. Fully aware of the newcomer, Toro knew beyond doubt that the moment required nothing from him. Bigger straightened to face the person negotiating his quarter mile of winding drive.

She was farther away than he expected. The long cast of her shadow reached the yard though she was still some distance from the gate. For an instant, he could take in only black curls framing her face and the onrushing colors of evening reflected in her eyes. She seemed, at first, to have no scale, and—for an instant, as if his vision faltered—she seemed only abstractly human, more tendency than shape, like a walking elemental. A trick of the light, he decided.

She looked around as she approached, ignoring Bigger. The old frame farmhouse with its afterthought additions drew her scrutiny, as did the long, low structure of bays and workshop that it faced across the yard. Her critical eye paused on the lean-to bump of his chickenhouse, then danced over tarp-covered forms of the hand-built pedal cars.

From where he watched, she seemed to walk out of the moon. Huge and red behind her, its nearly full face kissed an arc of horizon free of the turbulent clouds that claimed the setting sun. Rising defiantly, the moon cast gold and purple onto the advancing belly of the storm. Colors thrown back by the clouds spilled into the woman's moonshadow, shifting across him with the sway of her hips.

The strange light dazzled Bigger, making her hard to behold. She registered, first, as a series of impressions: a small woman, no taller than his chest. Hair so black it gleamed blue in the highlights. Skin like coffee with cream. She wore an unadorned shift, white, sleeveless, plain to the point of stark, but woven seamlessly, impossibly, of gossamer. Catching her as he watched, rain molded the garment to her body, making it clear that she wore nothing else.

When the first drops pelted down, the dogs rose from their sprawl near the repair bay and crossed the yard, mounting the steps to the porch. This in itself told Bigger something about the woman. Normally they would have been at his side, and stayed close until he sent them to cover. Not now. Far from challenging the stranger, they had, in fact, walked away. While he waited in the rain, the dogs sheltered on the porch, pressed against the shiplap siding of the house where only the strongest gusts managed to wet them.

His visitor was indifferent to the effect of the downpour on her clothing and equally indifferent to the effect she had on him. Were it not for the chickens, he might have stayed frozen, eyes fixed on her every step. The noisy distress of his birds, however, broke her spell, and he swung around to see why they were still in the weather.

His alpha hen, Jefita, sat squarely in the opening of the coop, looking on as the rest of the flock dithered wet and distressed. Unwilling to challenge her, the other hens huddled miserably, cackling their upset.

"Hey!" Bigger snapped at Jefita. "Move it!"

The hen settled herself more resolutely, but otherwise did not react. Bigger scooped a stone from the yard and fired it side-armed into the wind-gong bonging softly above the door of the coop. The missile struck with a clang! that drove Jefita flapping backward into the chickenhouse. He tallied the other birds as they filed in. The little ruddy hen, his wanderer, was absent. She would have to wait. Bigger turned back to the drive.

The woman was through the gate, as if she had leapt forward when he wasn't looking.

Drenched, her shift clung, all but transparent, a quality of her skin more than a dress. She ignored this, making no move to hide her breasts visible through the sheer fabric. Even dry the insubstantial material would have hidden little of what lay beneath, though it was obviously tougher than it looked, and she wore it with unconcern. The single item that she carried, she carried low, perhaps coincidentally, perhaps not, where it lent a sop to modesty.

Glancing to see what she held, Bigger's sight was arrested by a finely carved wooden chest. Though hardly larger than a shoebox, the weight of it pulled down her shoulders and caused her to lean forward as she walked. The textured relief of its wooden surfaces seemed to rush across the distance between them, filling his vision. Unimposing in size, it was still an insistent presence. Around it, he imagined condensing vapors of power and gravitas. He stood transfixed as step by step she carried the object into the yard.

The woman scrutinized him, assessing from the ground up. Bigger was aware of this peripherally, but could not look away from the box she held. Its detail grew increasingly clear as she brought it closer. Lightning flashed directly overhead with a resounding crack that returned him to the world in which he stood gawking. Rain tunneled cold down the back of his neck into his sopping shirt. His eyes flicked to her breasts and then to her face. Failing to decode her expression, he dropped his gaze again to the box.

Shaped like a miniature treasure chest, its body and arched lid were bound with iron bands. Unadorned, the bands contrasted with the elaborately chiseled wood. Even from a distance, the materials looked ancient. The oiled grain of the wood shone as if burnished by generations of touch. When the woman drew closer, he saw carved chest to chest across the box's front two standing bulls with human heads. The heads faced out, as though watching him.

Bigger was no anthropologist, but he was a wide-ranging reader of science. On that basis and no more, he thought the design Mesopotamian. If not a scientist, though, he was both an artisan and a careful observer, and he saw with certainty the box was an epitome of craft. As with the woman's shift, balanced lines and invisible seams were tokens of perfection. By reflex, he assumed it was a reproduction, a re-creation of some lost or degraded original. A late copy, it had to be. That a wooden artifact in such perfect state might have survived from Sumer or Akkad was inconceivable.

Still, his eyes told him, that even if a copy it was very old, and surpassing fine. The rain beading on its polished surface could not be good for it, yet the woman approached without haste, stepping with sure feet as the downpour ran in sheets over the cinder drive. She paid no more heed to the rain on the box than upon her shift.

These thoughts formed and passed. His eyes flickered back and forth from the box to all of her, assembling a sense of her appearance from details. Backlit by the huge Rose Moon, she fixed him with eyes that he could only tell were on him from the glint of their highlights. She came purposefully, gracefully through the storm.

Her sopping hair framed her face with black curls. Skirting those eyes lost beneath her brows, he followed the high curve of her cheeks to the bow of her lips, then shot decorum and stared at the shift molded to her small, erect breasts. Desire came in a flood. Bigger looked away, observing her in his peripheral vision. This made him very aware of her hips swinging side-to-side from a slender waist. She walked with a motion that made his mouth go dry. He licked rain-soaked lips.

She still watched him closely. Her head tilted as she closed, emphasizing the difference in their heights. He measured a hair under two meters, a little more if one allowed for the waves of his carrot top and its sprangs of premature gray.

Bigger imagined himself as she saw him, a round-shouldered figure in overalls, no longer young, not yet middle-aged, still lean, a dusting of freckles beneath the hard-won tan of his face. He straightened.

A grin plucked at her mouth and faded.

At last their eyes met.

He saw her brow lift when she registered the pale, liquid green of his irises. All his life he had heard how unusual they were, how beautiful and frightening. Her surprise made him self-conscious. He dropped his gaze, but caught by the pull of her body, he looked back at her face. She continued peering up, looking for some unknown in his expression.

The doubled, two-against-two rush of his heartbeat swelled in his ears.

"Mr. MacGregor?"

She stopped before him, waiting for acknowledgement. Bigger stared at her moving lips, but said nothing. Doubting suddenly, she looked around, apparently hopeful someone else might appear.

"Bigger MacGregor?" she tried again.

Tossing her chin, she indicated the legend painted on the outside of the fabrication bay.

"MacGregor Pedal Cars. Mr. MacGregor is here, yes?"

"Yes," Bigger echoed vacantly, then roused as though coming awake.

He closed his eyes and opened them, shuddering off the distraction of her presence. She shifted the box to one hand, swiping a curl behind an ear with the other.

Again he said softly, "Yes," then squared his shoulders and spoke too loudly, "Yes! I'm Bigger MacGregor."

The sudden boom of his voice embarrassed him, and he ducked his head, blushing.

"I'm sorry. You're the first woman with an invisible dress to walk out of the moon this week. My manners were overthrown."

He wiped a hand on his overalls and extended it.

"Please, come inside."

She ignored his hand with a tic of distaste.

Inclining her head to point, she advised, "My car. It is out in the lane. It has ceased to function."

Metrical and sibilant, her accent was definite but unplaceable. Though her words were precise, shifting consonants told him English was not her mother tongue.

The depth of her stare made him wonder if the present was her native time.

"Your car?" he mouthed, groping for his thoughts.

Bigger went up on his toes and craned his neck to scan the dirt road that crossed his property. At first he saw no sign of a vehicle, neither at the turn-in, nor along the graded cut that led toward town. When he spotted the canopy, it peeked over tall grass from near where the roadway ended, unofficially, among washouts and loose cobbles on the slope of Standing Rock.

"Ah! I see it," he told her. "You missed the turn-in? I'm surprised there was room to turn around."

"No."

The shake of her head was a single twitch.

"I drove straight here."

"You came over the rock?" he asked, incredulous. "Maps say there's road, but I can't remember the last time anyone tried it. You made it in a pedal car?"

"Mr. MacGregor!"

For an instant, she looked like she might hit him.

"May we discuss this somewhere out of the rain? Preferably after my car is under shelter?"

Her words stung, not least because he deserved it. From first sight of her, he had been, in a very real way, almost thoughtless. He struggled to recover.

"Oh, right. Right! You're drenched," he stated the obvious. "Listen. Go left on the porch to the hot tub. The robe hanging there is clean. I put it there last night, fresh from the wash. Make yourself comfortable in the house while I see about your car. Tea things are in the kitchen. Kettle's on the stove."

Balancing the box on her hip with one hand, she passed him without another word or look. Her other hand swung free in time with her steps. Bigger shielded his eyes and watched her saunter, unhurried, through the curtain of rain. He made himself turn away before she climbed the steps to his house.

His guest out of sight, the weather exploded upon his attention. Arriving at the same time she had, the rain had been a background detail, a condition of environment to note in memory of the moment: "When first I laid eyes on her, the sky was falling." It had been many months since a storm like this had raged. Already sodden, it was pointless to worry about rain gear for himself; there was, however, a need to protect the woman's car.

"Customer!" he corrected the framing of his thought. Transparent dress or not, she was a customer.

He detoured through the repair bay for his road kit and a tarp.

"And I'm a professional," he mumbled.

Water ran inches deep over the cinders of his drive. The rain drove down faster than the landscape could direct it. Bigger splashed gamely along the curves of the driveway, but slowed where mud made the footing less secure in the lane beyond.

Reaching the vehicle, he found that its driver had made no effort to pull off the road, for which he silently praised her. Had she pulled off, or even pulled too far to the right, the car would have mired beyond hope of one man moving it alone. Tracks told him she was hewing to the grassy crown at the center of the lane when she stopped. Four fat, all-terrain bike tires resting on the vegetated center promised that mud would not be his primary challenge.

The machine was fully enclosed, a custom two-seat coupe with a sculpted body and hatches mounted to swing up and forward. Bigger threw the folded tarp onto the roof and opened the driver's side. A hand on the steering grips, he put his shoulder to the hatch frame, bracing his feet on the muddy grass in the middle of the road. The car rocked forward when he shoved, but did not roll. A check of the levers showed that neither parking brake nor wind anchors were set.

"I was afraid of that," he muttered, grabbing the tarp.

With a flip of his wrists, the fabric snapped and spread, dropping onto the cab. Even though weighted around its perimeter, getting the tarp settled evenly over the car in a gusting storm took both effort and comment.

At last, he worried it into a position that allowed him to open the hatch fully without exposing the interior to wet.

Leaning to release the driver's seat and flip it out of the way, he popped the latch and froze. The seat's retraction mechanism was almost identical to the one in his cars. The efficient, economical fold of the parts had been one of his cleverer designs. Clever enough that he held a patent, granted three years before on a provisional basis and wending its way through treaty conventions of the North American successor states. Wear on the latches and pedals suggested the vehicle was about that old.

A closer look at the apparatus of curves and pivots revealed proportions differing slightly from his. The hardware was more gracile, more elegant. He shifted the seat back and forth, watching the interplay of parts. It was his design, but improved. The look suggested a copy from his very first production model, stolen almost day one. He knew every manufacturer with a license, and none of them had modified the shape and movement in this way. A quick inspection of the cabin showed no obvious maker's mark. Thunder reminded him of his immediate purpose. He set aside the mystery to puzzle out later, in a sheltered location and a drier time.

Raising the cowl over the drive-train, however, revealed new surprises. A variety of linkages between pedals and shaft were current in human-powered transport, but instead of one of those he found a row of flywheels. It was clearly a yoked sequence, but constructed in such a way that he could not tell how momentum transferred from one to the next.

Testing the nearest wheel with a finger, he found that it turned silently, without detectable resistance. Its neighbor began to counter-rotate at half the speed. When the next crept into motion, spinning the same direction as the first, he laid his hand over the array so the moving wheels brushed to a halt.

Bigger would have probed further, but a gust found its way under the tarp to remind him, again, that he was cold and wet. Curiosity buttoned, he released a latch his fingers found under the flywheels, and swung them out of the way on an assembly like that of the seat. Beneath were three jointed shafts in parallel and a fourth askew, broken at a coupling.

The intact joints of the unbroken shafts were as incomprehensible to him as the mechanics of the flywheels. That such shapes could do anything did not seem possible. If the functionability of the parts was a mystery, however, the effect of the break was not. An arm of the damaged coupling had snapped loose and wedged among the other shafts, preventing them from turning.

He added "parse the linkage" to an accumulating list of oddities this car would require him to figure out. For the moment, he pried loose the jam, pulled a cable-tie from his kit and secured the broken piece away from the other shafts. The wheels, happily, would now roll. Quickly rearranging the tarp so that he could see through the windshield, he put a shoulder back to the hatch frame and pushed the car up the drive to his yard.

The full fury of the storm burst as he left the repair bay. Rain, heavy before, now came down with painful force, its angle changing unpredictably with the wind.

In passing, he scooped the little wandering hen from its miserable huddle beneath the scant protection of a sumac, tucked her into the crook of an elbow, and dashed to the house.

The dogs rose when he stomped up the steps, and crowded close to enter with him as he pulled open the screen. This was unusual. In most weather, even the foulest, Toro and Belle chose to shelter on the porch or in the open bays. A feral pack ranged the area, and not infrequently had to be discouraged from breaching the fence. If his dogs pressed to get out of the weather, this blow, bad as it was, would likely get worse.

Lightning strikes came one after another, marching close. Thunderclaps rattled the house. His hair prickled from the ionized air as he pushed through the door, the dogs brushing past into dry warmth. Bigger released the hen into a nest box kept in the entry for such moments, slid the overalls straps from his shoulders and pulled off his shirt.

With a nod of thanks, he accepted a towel the woman held waiting. She retreated, turning her back as he dried his face. He paused, eyeing the shape her figure gave his terry-cloth robe.

"What's your name?"

She went stiff at the sound of his voice, apparently surprised that he addressed her.

"What do I call you?"

"Eanna," she answered without turning. "You may call me Eanna."

He waited to see if there was more.

Still without facing him, she added, "You should get out of those wet things, Mr. MacGregor. You are courting a chill."

Quickly, he stripped off the rest of his clothing. Towel knotted at waist, he hurried for the shower.

***

When Bigger emerged in drawstring pants and a T-shirt, he found he still confronted the back of his guest. Belle crouched at the front door, staring fixedly, as though expecting someone or something to come through. He spotted Toro lying on the rug near the kitchen, head between forelegs but eyes open, positioned where he could watch the other doors into the room, and all the windows. The big dog spared him a look, flicked a glance to the woman, then sank back into his own alert counsel. Belle never stirred.

Eanna stood close to a wall, hugging herself, flinching at the thunder and lightning. Hanging where she faced was a circular plaque, a small hand cast in plaster, bright pink except for a name, Rebecca, in a child's scratch and colored turquoise, below the palm. Corners where the wallpaper had not faded stuck out behind the plaque, marking an absent rectangle, perhaps something framed, like a photo. Bigger came no closer, watching her reach out as though to cover the cast with her own hand, but she jerked back at a flash to the west that threw stark shadows from momentarily brilliant details of the room. Another, to the northeast, lit her terry-clad form, sparking rainbows and highlights in the black tangle of her hair.

She was shaking. At first he thought she wept, but she did not. Trembling, not weeping, gripped her, although the violence of the shivers wrung her out in shallow panting much like sobs.

Bigger stopped before reaching her.

"Eanna?"

She spun at his voice. Eyes wide and body taut, she vibrated with intensity that matched the storm.

"The old one is angry!" She cried. "He cannot see, but he knows I am near."

The dark outside was ripped away, only to collapse back upon the house beneath a blast of thunder. She half crouched, finally looking at him directly.

"Shutters!" she demanded. "Are there shutters?"

"Yes!"

Bigger jumped to show her.

"They just crank shut. I made them myself. Come on."

Eanna made no move from beneath the plaque. Bigger went to each window in turn, cranking closed the accordion-fold shutters in the room where she stood, and then throughout the house. Returning, he found she still half-crouched, still hugged herself, still trembled.

Lightning came, a chaotic volley, so close one after another that the ground beneath them shuddered. Between crashes of thunder, the wind carried snatches of baying and howls from the feral pack. Bigger thought it strange they had not gone to ground with the storm. They were faint through the din, but drawing closer.

Eanna's head shifted. She heard them also.

"Not to worry," Bigger joked. "The house may creak, but most of the construction is solid. We're all set for tempest, flood and savage beast."

She ignored him as though he had not spoken, her head turned rigidly away. She stared, apparently through wall and distance, at the running pack.

"Eanna?"

When she did not respond, Bigger moved into her line of sight. Terror and fascination warred across her face. She peered at him as from a great distance. Sinking to her knees, she spoke, her voice husky.

"He knows that I have what he has lost."

Beads of sweat stood out on her forehead.

"I am veiling us as best I can, but he knows I am close. He eats away at me!"

Bigger knelt beside her. He took her hand to clasp, but she snatched it away and clung more tightly to herself.

"It's a storm," he assured her. "It's just energy churning in the atmosphere."

Looking away, she muttered through gritted teeth. The language was not English.

"It's a storm," he soothed. "It will pass."

She inhaled prodigiously. Shaking her head, Eanna opened her mouth to answer, but before words emerged, lightning struck in a cascade. Like hammer blows, behind the house, in front and to the side, the flashes blasted through the slits of the shutters like an eruption of blue-white into the world.

Bigger froze, all the hair of his body standing on end from the charge in the air, but the triple blasts drove Eanna onto him. Clamping him with her thighs, the borrowed robe falling open, she grabbed Bigger's head in both her hands.

"He eats away at me!" she shouted.

"Who eats at you?"

Bigger's hands came up to cover hers.

"Who is here besides us?"

"The old one."

The words seemed to tear out of her throat.

"He pulls at the veil. We must throw him off. Kiss me!"

"What?"

Bigger gulped, perplexed.

Eanna's features softened. She released him and stepped away, looking anywhere but at his face. Her fleeting shyness departed an instant later. Seeing him without the formless cloak of his overalls, she registered the plunging vee of his shoulders to hips. Almost smiling, she brushed at the furrow in his brow with her thumb.

"Through my thoughts of him, he sees."

Her voice was low and coarse, as from fever.

"He is lost if my mind turns away."

Slowly, Eanna lifted her chin to confront his still bewildered look.

She added, unblinking, "Please. Kiss me."

Though the request was startling, her earnestness drew him forward. Bigger parted his lips to respond, but her mouth covered his, her tongue a grace note, flicking to touch spit to his spit and retreat. Like a switch was thrown, he fell into the kiss as into another world. The external environment rushed away, leaving her contact, her scent growing musky and hot like primordial vapor. Her mouth on his mouth.

He plunged into silence. Sound retreated as though swept away. Her mouth on his mouth, that was the whole of being. Her tongue touched his tongue, had always touched his tongue. Never had his mouth not sealed to her mouth.

Slowly, into the muffled absence came a pulse, two-against-two, familiar, far off but surging rapidly closer. All at once the beat overrode the storm and rushed into the world, pounding, the cycles of a titanic engine.

Another sound, too, defied the rattle and blast. A low, shifting fundamental, a deep tectonic note, swelled and faded.

In stop-motion, he lifted his head to gasp for air.

At first he did not recognize the enormous pulse as his beating heart, nor the soughing as his breath. When he realized that the great noise blanketing his senses was the song of his own life, his hearing pierced it. He heard the heaving breath of other lungs and felt on his ribs the pounding of a heart through another's chest. Two-against-two, the rhythm was not his but reacted to his, the doubled beat of hers faster, insistent, a call and a response putting spurs to his imagination. The throb beneath her breasts paced his in counterpoint.

Eanna swung her face expectantly toward him. Half wary that she might turn away, he swam forward, but her mouth opened readily to the exploration of his tongue. She pulled blindly at his clothing as his arms encircled her, one within her robe, one without. Feeling muscles twitch beneath his fingertips, he traced down the small of her back with his inside hand, following the belling curve to her thigh. She molded to him. Bigger rose, swept her up and bore her forward to the couch. He tore loose from her arms to strip off his shirt.

She watched, unflinching, the parted robe a frame to her body. Her chest rose and fell as he stared into her, eye for eye, and rose and fell still as he drank in her form. Unconsciously, he licked his own lips at the swelling sight of hers. Bigger licked again at the sight of her breasts, small, round, nipples erect. His mouth went completely dry when his gaze descended the curves of her belly to the manicured hair at the join of her legs.

Lowering to the floor in front of her, he placed a hand inside each of her knees and parted them. His eyes again sought hers as he moved into the wedge of space. Eanna grew still, giving him no sign. He leaned to kiss her, and she pressed upward, responding, but this time he did not allow her to lock into it. The play of his mouth on hers was glancing, a provocative nibble, a feint as his hand slowly traveled the inside of her thigh.

With gentle, circular motion, he massaged ever higher on her leg until the saddle of his palm found the cleft at her center. He felt her grow moist, and pressed there as he descended, kissing beneath her chin, then the hollow of her throat. Opening his mouth wide to caress her breast, tongue at her nipple, he began to shift his hand to slowly press and release the hot swell of her response.

She gripped him with her thighs when the tip of his finger entered her. He nibbled her other breast, then kissed down her torso until she clenched tight to slow him. Bigger flexed his arms and dropped, pushing her legs apart so he could dive for the tender flesh high on her groin. He plucked the soft skin lightly with his teeth.

Again he slid the tip of his finger inside her, but now, little by little, he worked it deeper. Up and down, a feather's touch, his thumb traced the folds where his fingers pressed. Pushing lower, he slowly forced his elbows apart, spreading her legs wide. Eanna drew them up, raising her pelvis insistently to his touch. Bigger probed and stroked with finger and thumb until she began to push back. She growled when he withdrew his hand, but made an altogether different sound when he pressed his face between her legs to the fork. He drew the pale, vulnerable skin between his lips and released it with a pop. Once, twice, to the left first, then to the right. His nose took her scent. He paused, the stubble of his cheek against the satin flesh of her upper thigh.

Eanna shuddered at the prickling of his chin, pulling her leg away. Bracing a foot on Bigger's hip, she wriggled more solidly onto the couch. Her right hand blindly seized and released handfuls of his hair, laboring in time with her breathing. She moaned, a grudging, nearly silent guttural.

A twitch of his neck plunged him afresh into her scent. Bigger opened his mouth wide to cover the moist seep of her vulva. Following his finger, he reached his tongue inside her, though as his finger slipped farther in, his tongue slid upward to lap higher more than deep. With tiny thrusts, he pushed a second finger to join the first. Eanna bucked and squirmed. He shoved the fingers inside her to the knuckles. Tongue and lips sealed to her warm, moist flesh, he began to suck.

His heart pounded like walking mountains, an entire range in lock-step to the ferocious in-and-out of his breath. Eanna gasped at air, now slower, now fast. Bigger sucked and kissed and nibbled and licked, learning her pleasure, reflecting it. Time dilated. She drew her legs wider. When he reached the exquisite lesson of her aroused clit, he studied diligently until she pushed him off. He pressed back, lower, licking into her, stretching his tongue as far as it would reach. Eanna snatched his hair in both hands, and bellowed. His finger probed deep inside her, straining, until he curled it back to massage her vaginal wall. He sucked as he probed, and tongued up and down.

Her tension shifted. Eanna went limp, not in surrender but to better envelop, curling her back with her legs high. Bigger began slowly to rotate his fingers inside her. He twisted one way as he pushed deep, the other as he pulled back. Surprised, Eanna gasped, but caught on, and countered each twist with a flex of her hips. He pushed faster, bobbing, and began to suck in earnest. Her hands slapped onto his head, one to push him away; the more powerful pulling him tight.

Peaking, she snapped her legs up, locking his head. With both hands, she grasped his skull and pulled, forcing his face into her crotch. She kicked as she spasmed with pleasure. Bigger continued to suck, his fingers still stroking and probing, although with his nose forced against the bottom swell of her belly, he found it hard to breathe. His distress became acute when a second climax followed her first and she pulled his face tighter, squeezing her legs around his head like a vise. The sound of his heart in his ears rose again as his breathing choked to a wheeze.

Pulling both hands free, he tried first to pry her legs from his head, but she had gone rigid. His position gave him no leverage. He slapped her legs and arms, but she was oblivious. The strain in his chest became agony as he fought to pull more air into the strangled pipe of his respiration. It was not enough. Slipping from consciousness, he heard, coming through her body, a scream of outraged joy as Eanna swept to a third peak. Bigger fell into black, unaware too swiftly to have caught from outside the house the final, pattering staccato of departing rain.

II

She blew on his eyelids to wake him. Bigger flinched, and blinked.

Their location shifted. Light fell upon them from the open door to the bedroom, blood-colored rather than the soft white of the house LEDs. They knelt facing each other, between them the unexplained wooden chest.

Eanna spoke, but the words were incomprehensible. Bigger could not tell whether her speech was broken up or that she spoke an unknown language. The sound of her voice fractured, as though colliding with another, distinct existence.

She waited expectantly for a response. When he did not react, she spoke again. He watched her lips, hoping for a clue to what she said. When he still did not respond, she rocked forward and deftly flipped open the chest.

The lid blocked his view of the insides, but not of the blue-white pulse shining onto her from the recess. She rummaged in the contents and took out a small, luminous object pinched between finger and thumb. She turned it, a cube glowing dimly from within, inspecting it carefully.

Nothing about the appearance of the object made sense to him, not its texture or its color. It changed as she turned it, seeming, from some angles, less than completely material.

A phrase, "compressed light," came to him unbidden.

"Yes," he murmured.

That caught it. A leaky cube of compressed light.

Eanna spoke again, her tone soothing. She rocked forward, off her heels, rising upright on her knees to push

29

the object against his forehead. He had a fleeting sense of pressure at the hollow above his brow, and then a jolt as the object passed into his skull.

His eyes opened wide, and he fell away from her into unbounded space. Darkness swarmed toward him, closing first to enwrap and then draw him down. Bigger tumbled backward, head over heels. He felt the object inside his head decompress, expanding while he fell. He felt, too, an itch spreading as precise tendrils snaked from it to trace his axons. An aura he could not observe, visible in afterthought, visible only in the signature of its travel, diffused along his synapses. A million impossible colors flickered into his awareness. There was something he knew as the aura spread, coded in the sensing of it. A knowledge was becoming his, as if innately, although knowledge of what he could not say.

His tumbling became a slow roll, himself a mote adrift in vast convections. The boundlessness knit around him, mirrored in his breast by a contented flush. At a moment he did not observe, Bigger's fall transformed into a rocking motion. His descent ceased, or became imperceptible. He rocked, clasped to the bosom of being, thinking nothing. His respiration slowed. Soothed by the hum of his own atoms, he folded into stillness.

***

Either the sound of the door woke him, or he imagined the sound of the door when he woke. Bigger lay atop the covers. Though he strained to hear, he knew at once that no one else was in the house. It took only a minute to rise and confirm that he was alone. The robe Eanna had worn hung from a hook on the bathroom door. The chest, an enigma his hands twitched to open, sat on his dining table, evidence that his absent guest had not been a phantom.

Tangible but uninformative, the box drew him. Its man-headed bulls watched when he stopped in the doorway, and watched when, curious but also wary, he started forward.

A step into the room, he caught a fleet whiff of her musk. Sniffing right, then left, he chased it, then realized it came from his own skin. The ancient casket was almost forgotten when he placed a hand atop it. This object and the smell of her juices laid bare her absence.

Even flirting with melancholy, however, he was pricked by guilt. He had a friend. They had never talked about what they were to each other, or defined boundaries, but things between them were easy. Warm and easy. And close. Not often, but often enough.

Bigger pulled his phone from a pocket of his overalls, and tapped "Q-U." The directory autofilled "Quella," and sang numbers as it dialed, but as soon as it finished, the screen announced, "Signal Lost," and went dark. He tried twice more with the same result. The storm, he decided, must have damaged a tower. Maybe that was good. Maybe there were no grounds for an awkward conversation.

An afterthought, he realized his free hand still rested on the box.

Bigger imagined information flowing from the carved wood under his palm, an explanation for Eanna's presence and absence that he could not decipher. Suddenly, he flushed hot. To wake and find her gone! She was not there to face him, or for him to face. There had been no morning after, unless, but, no. That had been a dream. The things that happened, the falling, the cube of light, those could exist only in dream. A substantial dream, but a dream nonetheless.

Probing with a finger told him the depression just above his brow actually was tender to the touch. Likely she had bopped his head when it was gripped between her thighs. He was ready to believe it. He was ready to believe almost anything. Her absence was a canvas onto which he could project his ignorance of who she was and from where she had come.

His budding resentment gave way, if grudgingly, before a growing suspicion that during the night he had learned something. It was like knowledge he could not yet see directly had come as he slept. Possibly a change of context, or perspective. An axiom onto which he could not put a finger.

Drawing away from the box, he returned to the bedroom for clean overalls. The lesson he could not quite describe asserted itself. Physical memory of her legs gripping his skull suggested lines of motion and pivots. Her scent upon him evoked visions of an idealized machine. Shirtless and in flipflops, he left the house.

In the yard, his eyes went first to the three-wheeler he had been securing when Eanna arrived. Blasted scrap from a lightning strike was all that remained. His fingers twitched, remembering when he built it.

Toeing a lump of charred carbon among the wreckage, he glanced around to see what other losses he had suffered. There was no obvious destruction, but a bicycle was gone from the rack under the shop awning. An augmented off-road bike, it was a better fit for pounding up gullies than for a leisurely ride to town. Whether or not there was significance in Eanna's choice of ride, he could only wonder.

The three-wheeler was nearly a complete loss. This was not a conclusion Bigger reached casually. Among home shops, handmakers like himself, the man behind MacGregor Pedal Cars was famous for finding usable material in the most picked-over waste stream. Once, on a bet, he had created a two-seat four-wheeler entirely from cast-offs of a bicycle chop shop. He had done a lot of that as a kid, cutting corners on the fly.

In this case, what had not burned to ash was nonetheless charred. He managed to dig out small pieces of slag, all that remained of the gears and derailleur. When he went to slip the pieces into his overalls pocket, they clung to the button.

"Magnetized," he thought. "That's interesting."

Bigger would save the pieces apart from other scrap. "Lightning charged," he named them.

The three-wheeler was the only hit to inventory. An elm sapling near the repair bay had splintered to its roots, and on the far side of the house a roughly circular spot had been blasted bare. The exposed soil had partially melted. A morning breeze, still cool, picked up as he prodded the glassy crust with the toe of a flipflop. Absently, he lifted his chin to dry sweat from the line of his throat and neck.

Turning to go on around the house, he stopped at sight of the lightning rods on his roof. Not one appeared to have taken a hit. No blackened points, no new kinks, nothing to suggest the bolts had struck the attractors first and leapt to the ground. Another old tale disproved, he decided. Lightning did what it would do. In his pocket was proof of that.

Also untouched was Eanna's car. Guy wires secured it from winds that may have swept the partly open bay. The tarp remained dry and taut, and came off to expose the material presence of the coupe in mute contrast to absence of the driver. Through the flexiplex side window, he imagined a glimpse of her, the way she distributed herself in the driver's sling. He saw, for a flash, the angle of her feet on the pedals, her hands on the grips of the steering crescent and the shift.

Bigger tapped his temples to clear his thoughts. She was not there and the car was. So be it.

Popping the left-side hatch, he pulled a stool alongside the opening and perched. Rather than going first to the obvious repair, he began an inspection of the vehicle at the driver's seat. Like most of the rest of the car, its frame was molded fiber composite. The sling, however, was leather, a material he never used. Imperfections in the surface proved it was from an animal, nothing vat grown. He fingered a scar high on the seat back. Here was evidence tanned forever into this hide that a pain had healed crudely. Leaning close, he scented her trace embedded in the tanned animal smell. His hand grew warm when he rested it in the cup of the sling shaped by her laboring butt.

Bigger stood and closed the hatch. Dogs and chickens were ready for breakfast, and he wanted coffee. Prudence called for shoes and a t-shirt. His calendar was open. The rest of the day lay before him once the animals were fed.

***

By mid-afternoon, he decided the seat mechanism was likely coincidence, an independent discovery of the same principle as his own. An elegant independent discovery. No maker's mark or patent stamp appeared on any part of the seat, nor anywhere else in the vehicle as far as he could tell. He had looked in the likely places, curious, but with his mind elsewhere. Professional interest in the identity of the car's designer was of decidedly secondary importance. Even as he looked over the vehicle, his imagination combined and recombined features of this gracile assembly with the more robust lines of his own. Rapidly, methodically, he plotted steps to a hybrid.

The first spark of synthesis had come as he monkeyed with the carriage in which the flywheels sat. Bigger liked flywheels. Part of his reputation rested on the extraordinary efficiency of the "MacGregor Sandwich," a large flywheel flanked by smaller, counterspinning wheels on either side. The improvement in performance over previous technical standards resulted from his invention of a circular, double-helix worm gear that transferred and reversed motion between wheels in a single step. The patent had been his third, but the first to generate significant licensing revenues. It had made his name one to conjure with among designers around the world. Major manufacturers reverse engineered his new models within days of release. He was, word had it, a man inspired.

The array in Eanna's car had double the flywheels of the MacGregor Sandwich, all of a uniform size. Try as he might, he could not discover how the wheels interconnected within their nested sleeves and yokes— but in a flash he saw how to improve power transfer into and out of the array by modifying the retraction mechanism. An impression of Eanna's leg—hip, knee, ankle, the complexity of her feet— superimposed over the

34

shifting parts of the retractor as he watched it work. At once he saw which curves of the existing arrangement matched to which curves of his hybrid to reproduce the proportions of her leg. That the improvement applied to the seat design also was a side benefit.

A plan for a prototype took shape in his mind almost without direction. Bigger stood away from the car to let the idea sink in. Faint but startling, Eanna's scent surprised him. It dissipated instantly—if he had not just imagined it. Yearning, completely unexpected, flushed through him, clouding his mechanical visions. The world seemed to twist a degree, and he jerked back to catch his balance. The moment passed. Bigger looked at the pedal car and saw only a car.

"Break time," he decided.

Outside the bay, he paused to stretch, letting his eyes adjust to the light. Motion behind the steps to the house forced him to squint against the glare. The little red hen, his wanderer, paced the deep shade beneath the deck of the porch, hesitating every few steps with one leg lifted. She cocked her head with each pause to scrutinize particulars only she could see. It occurred to him that either he would crawl on his belly to collect her next clutch of eggs, or he would wait until she hatched the chicks and led them into the open herself.

Minutes later, iced tea in hand, Bigger lowered himself onto one of the chairs on the porch. A panting dog plopped on either side. Bigger crossed his ankles atop the railing and fidgeted to find a comfortable position against the chair back. His head lolled onto the top slat. Without really seeing, he watched barn swallows come and go from a trio of nests where ceiling met wall at the end of the porch. Breezes across the front of the house cooled the shade where man and dogs relaxed.

Bigger slipped lazily into planning a new retraction assembly, neatly ordering pieces he envisioned into a series of steps for lathe and tool bench. His eyes followed the swallows while his imagination scaled proportions and configured parts.

Silently, the picture in his head morphed as he worked through the mechanics of his concept. It was mental play that came naturally to Bigger. Unbidden, though, without notice, minute by minute, he drifted toward drowse in the hot afternoon. A voice at the back of his mind sang wordlessly, joyfully, of evolving shapes and slippages. Gradually, it lost any trace of sense and merged, one more voice, with the droning cicadas.

The heads of both dogs came up at once. Rage, almost inaudible, gargled deep in Toro's throat. Bigger shot to his feet, eyes sweeping the yard before he had shaken off his daydream. The dogs, ridges of hair standing from the crowns of their heads down their necks, rose beside him.

He started for the steps, but the dogs bumped him from either side, heading him off. Astonished, he looked down at Belle, not quite touching him. She gazed up, as though to make sure he understood he should not go forward. Toro leaned a shoulder into Bigger's leg, but stared toward the field beyond the open gate.

In a gesture strange and rare from the self-sufficient animal, Belle licked his hand, then turned her head slowly, deliberately, perhaps, even, signally, to face the same place as her brother. Bigger followed their stare. The head of a man out on the road bobbed into view from behind the shop building. The head popped in and out of sight beyond the field of tall grass and scrub between the road and the yard. Both dogs growled continuously.

When the man attached to the head reached the turnoff for the drive, he dropped from sight. Dogs shouldering him to stop, Bigger pushed to the top step, bracing against a post as he leaned out to see. The man was on all fours, taut on knuckles and toes to keep his clothes from being soiled, nose against the ground, sniffing. Bald and brown, he wore a belted tunic over baggy trousers—out of sync with prevailing fashion, Bigger silently observed.

Sniffing exploratorily, the man crept forward, shifting from side to side as he lifted and placed each limb separately and carefully, his flared nostrils testing the cinders over which they passed. Abruptly, he stopped, pushing up with his legs and shoving his face almost into the cinders. He snuffled ferociously at whatever scent he had struck. Satisfied at last, the man stood and continued up the drive.

Toro's howl rose from his chest. The sound that emerged was primeval, the declaration of an elemental. Her eyes showing wide, Belle joined her voice to his.

The man stopped just outside the gate. Bigger descended to the foot of the steps, the dogs crowding protectively in front of him. They pushed back hard when he tried to go forward, so he stopped and eyed the stranger from across the yard.

It was not so much that the man was bald, he was completely hairless. Not even eyelashes broke his skin. His complexion was the same coffee with cream as Eanna's. In fact, as Bigger watched the man, he saw flitting resemblance to his absent guest. A not-quite-identifiable expression. A stance vaguely familial. Like half-siblings? Uncle and niece? Shouldering hard against his legs, the dogs moaned when Bigger pushed a few yards closer.

The man's attention fixed on Toro. In no way did he acknowledge the person trying to confront him, but he watched the dog closely. After a moment, he made a tutting sound to the unresponsive animal, and smiled. Bigger recoiled. The man's mouth held too many teeth. Dozens too many.

Gravity seized hold of Bigger and grew titanically, until he was swallowed in a well of his own mass. With every particle of will, he fought to keep from sinking immobilized to earth. Torpor descended over his thoughts, which thickened like agar, and his vision contracted to a small, bright focus on those teeth.

It was as though that bizarre mouth was a hypnotist's watch, draining vigor from his mind. A sensation, like webworms spinning, pricked in his brain. He resisted. There was a protocol to follow, and protocol was focus.

He shook his head with a snap, ripping the mental lint.

"May I help you?" he demanded curtly.

The man ignored this overture too, sighting along a line the gate had dragged across the cinders when it slid opened and closed. He looked at Toro, leaned forward, and, smiling again, said something incomprehensible. The utterance may or may not have been words; it was impossible to tell. His voice sounded like he spoke bubbles underwater.

"Speaking beneath oceans of air."

The phrase pronounced carefully in Bigger's inner voice. Immediately, the notion projected backward to the night before, to the...dream?...of falling. He had tumbled in an ocean of air.

Some part of the association held a clue to this interloper, Bigger was sure. It was a signifier he needed to hold until his head cleared, until he could think.

Whatever the man had said, Toro's ear twitched. This did not go unnoticed by Belle, whose sharp "woof" was a controlled explosion. Toro stomped his forefeet and lowered his head, leaving no doubt about his reaction. A snarl rippled the big dog's muzzle. Chuckling, the hairless man straightened. He said something more to Toro, and waved a placative hand, but the dog was not mollified. The man chuckled again, turned and began to make his way along the drive, back toward the road.

The dogs threw themselves hard against Bigger, driving him toward the house.

"Hey, wai—!" he cried, fighting to keep his balance.

The dogs were insistent. He had to dance away from the gate before they allowed him to recover. Both animals calmed as Bigger regained his balance.

He checked the drive, then walked its length to look up and down the road. There was no sign of the man.

Coming back to the yard, he found the little wandering hen pecking grit at the open gate. Bigger scooped her up, as much from the habit of carrying her as anything, and deposited her near the chicken house on his way back to the repair bay.

***

The linkage of the broken shaft came free when he was not paying attention. His mind had wandered back to the peculiar man when a half-unconscious flex of his fingers slipped the assembly from its barrel. For a moment he could only stare at the interslotted pieces of metal and ceramic. His hands replayed their movements in pantomime before the release action became clear to him: a double release, like a Chinese finger trap. Retract first, then slide out.

He recognized the other end of the shaft as an elongated version of the same design. It was a clever approach that should have allowed all the parts to slip freely any way except loose. That the assembly had, in fact, slipped loose suggested a problem with the... There. A ceramic slot was rough-ground to double width, allowing the jointed steel finger that rode it to escape. He found the cause of the wear in a burr on one steel edge, a tempered flaw that scraped at the slot every time the finger ran through its motion.

Once he understood the parts, he began to trace how they functioned together. Working out elements in combination, he guided the shaft through its action, using pressure from his palm to keep the burred piece from jumping the damaged slot. Motion traveled the length of the assembly in a multi-jointed wave, the steel rocking at a sequence of pivots to transfer energy in a regular, toroidal pulse along its length. Bigger found the movement eerily biological, and racked his brain for an elusive memory. A memory from a lesson. A teasing, fleet memory of something specific in which once he had been instructed. It came back to him like a burst.

"Peristalsis!"

Thought of the man with too many teeth evaporated as Bigger MacGregor, designer, was snared by glimpses of new possibility. Inner and outer mechanisms nested with no fixed connection. Energy moved from one assembly to the other by peristaltic transfer. One segment spun the other not by turning it directly but by the rippling swell and contraction of its elongated cap. On close examination, inner and outer components of the shaft proved to twist slightly, almost imperceptibly, in complementary directions.

"Brilliant!" he thought.

An open, gradual spiral thus imparted to the motion would be sufficient to start and maintain spin; the undulations conveyed the force that drove the wheels.

A sigh from Toro, supine in the narrow shade at the front of the bay, drew the visionary from his clouds. It was a "heads up" sigh, a signal to pay attention to the world, which Bigger obligingly did. Backing from the vehicle's hatch, he rested a hand on the canopy as he arched his back to stretch out the kinks. He stood away from the car and twisted right and left to limber his spine after too long hunched over. Belle stuck her head around the corner and woofed.

"Coming!" he answered, sauntering from the bay while wiping his hands on a shop rag.

A thunderhead massed in the west, its inky bottom perched on the horizon. Hidden lightning threw its rapidly shifting shape into high relief. Billowing, its heights bulged orange and yellow from scarlet seams. The defiant palette of a retreating sun.

He watched rising cloud feed on the solar disk. It was an impressive sight, but not, he was sure, why the dogs had rousted him. Looking from the gathering storm, he saw Eanna at the gate, which she had closed.

Back to him, she rested her hands on the top rail. Her cut-offs and t-shirt were sweat-soaked. The bike she had ridden lay to one side. She muttered, quietly, but in guttural tones almost too raw to be language.

He could tell she was aware of him, but she did not interrupt herself to acknowledge that he hovered nearby. Instead, finishing her utterance, she laid her cheek on the top rail and sighted along the painted metal. Satisfied, she turned her head to sight along the opposite way. Only after seeing whatever she saw did Eanna stand and turn. She shoved wordlessly past him.

From the set of her shoulders, he knew she was angry—and wound tight. Tension radiated from her in waves. Bigger said nothing when she disappeared into the bay, and he chose to linger in the yard rather than trail after her. It did not seem an auspicious time to discuss her car. He heard her yank open the vehicle's rear hatch, wrest something from behind the seat, and slam the hatch shut. The suitcase she hefted when she emerged was large enough to make him curious about the compartment where it had ridden. Large enough also to make him wonder how long she intended to stay.

Part of him wanted to avoid confrontation and return to work on the vehicle, but his wiser mind prevailed. Instinct whispered that the longer he waited to touch off the explosion, the larger it would be. He could not help wondering which storm would spend more violence, the one boiling to existence in the sky or the other gaining strength inside his house.

As soon as he passed through the door he was ready to put money on the interior tempest. Wrapped in the terry robe, Eanna faced him across the open cavity of her wooden chest. Her eyes flashed fire as she slammed the lid and palmed something into her pocket. Bigger raised two fingers in a peace sign.

"Truce?" he asked. "Talk?"

In answer, she spun on her heel and stomped into the bathroom. He watched through the open door while she rummaged in a toiletries case. Having found what she sought, she rushed out, and would have gone past him, except he touched her shoulder.

"Eanna," he began. only to have her round on him, hands thrown up, hissing in rage.

This was more than he would take.

"Eanna!" he snapped. "What is wrong? Why in hell are you so mad?"

"Yes, hell!" she spat. "Hell is where you belong!"

Her anger struck like a blow. The fight he had steeled for was suddenly pointless. When he repeated his question, he sounded weary.

"What...," he began.

His hand moved unconsciously, in a stirring motion.

"What's wrong?"

She shoved at him, pushing herself away.

"No one!" she shouted. "No one has ever done that to me. Ever!"

Confusion made him hesitate before answering. She glared, her lips pressed tight.

"I'm sorry," he said at last, trying to feel his way slowly. "I should have asked first. I mean, I guess there was a whole discussion we should have had—"

"Don't be an idiot!" she fumed. "I say nothing about sex. No one has ever shown me such disrespect. No one!"

Bigger's confusion deepened.

"Are you upset that I passed out?"

He shook his head in disbelief.

"You squeezed so tight. I tried to make you let go. I couldn't breathe."

Eanna's expression softened reluctantly. She answered in a voice somewhat lower than a shout.

"You got what you deserved. On and on you went. No one has ever cost me so much control."

"Wait!"

Light went on in the MacGregor pate.

"You're pissed about having an orgasm?"

"Not one!" she snapped.

Smacking the bib of his overalls with force that may or may not have been playful, she repeated herself, softer, "Not just one. And then you slept."

Bigger scratched his head, aggravating cowlicks never combed out that morning. He blinked rapidly, as though the words she spoke made little sense.

Finally, he lifted his palms in surrender.

"This day is just too weird. First, the hairless guy with all the teeth, and now you want to gut me because...."

He trailed off as the look on her face changed from anger to mischief, and then distress. Bigger wet his lips and waited. Eanna tightened her arms across her chest.

When she said nothing, he pressed, "What is it?"

She glanced around, as though suddenly wary.

"What guy?" she asked.

Her voice was sharp, precise, but not loud.

"What guy with all the teeth?"

Bigger pinched the bridge of his nose. His brow knit as he thought back to the visitor. The tender spot on his forehead prickled, so he let go of his nose to rub there with the pad of his thumb. Trying to recall that mouth ghastly with teeth, he sighed, long and heavily, like an echo of Toro.

"I don't know what guy."

Recalling the encounter took more effort than it seemed it should. Bigger's thoughts grew sluggish, as though memory had turned thick, like mud and cold syrup. He had to fight to recall, as he had fought to think when the man was present.

"I was on the porch, taking a break from your car. The dogs woke me from a doze because this weird character turned off from the road. I was watching him come up the drive when he dropped out of sight. The dogs tried to keep me from going to see where he'd gone. Turned out, he was on all fours, sniffing the ground. Then up he hopped and came to the gate, but he stopped. He wouldn't come through. It was open, but he stopped right at the line in the dirt. The dogs crowded me all the way out to see what he wanted. They were unhappy when I tried to get close, but the guy acted like I wasn't there. Only Toro. He only paid attention to Toro, but Toro didn't like him. Belle just plain hated his guts."

Eanna placed a hand on Bigger's chest as he talked, resting it there without force. When he finished, she stared, eyes wide, at her nails against the denim of the overalls. The instant before he broke into her silence, her expression changed, becoming distant, bemused. She drummed fingers on the hem of his bib, nodding as though she still weighed his words. Finally, she gazed at him speculatively.

"What," she asked at last, "did you mean about his teeth? What about all of them?"

"That was…well…that was the gruesome thing."

Bigger struggled, as though pulling the memory through haze.

"Here was a totally hairless guy, dressed like Sinbad the sailor, talking to my dog. As he talked, it looked like he had too many teeth."

"Tell me," she insisted. "How do you mean?"

Self-conscious, Bigger lowered his voice.

"I mean, it looked like he had twice as many teeth as could possibly fit in his mouth. There was no way that many could be in there, but they were."

Too loudly, he added, "And they weren't little, either."

He stopped, waiting for her to scoff or offer an explanation. Eanna fiddled with the button on his bib pocket, and chewed absently at her lip. A rumble of thunder startled her from her thoughts. In the wake of the roll-off, they heard barking from the feral pack, distant but heading toward them. Toro stood, his growl seeming to come from everywhere. Belle paced before the door, hackles up.

"I cannot think of this," Eanna declared. Shoving his shoulder playfully, she told him, "You must bathe. Clean yourself, then we must act."

Bigger started to respond, but she pushed him harder.

"After," was all she said.

She turned and walked away, going to her box. Bigger watched her place her hands on its lid, and saw her attention fall inward. When it was clear she would say nothing else, he headed for the shower.

***

Hair dripping on his bare shoulders, he emerged from the bathroom to find neither Eanna nor the dogs. His call, "Hello!" was drowned by thunder noticeably closer than before. He started to check all the rooms, but stopped. The structure creaked with the gusting wind, but the stillness of the inside air made it clear he was alone.

Belle's "woof" greeted him when he stepped through the front door onto the porch. The dogs lay before the

44

screened enclosure of the hot tub. Heads up and ears erect, they looked out toward the coming storm. Bigger leaned to scratch between the ears of first Belle, then Toro. Each dog stretched its neck to receive the favor. Eanna spoke from the tub.

"There is not much time. The old one approaches."

Bigger straightened, and rested his hand on the ceramic knob of the screen door.

"The guy with the teeth, you mean?"

Before she could answer, Toro started to growl so low that it came up through the earth. Belle woofed again. It was her sharp, "pay attention" woof. Turning, Bigger saw the man with too many teeth standing beyond the gate, lips mouthing inaudible words. The intruder waved a stick as he spoke.

"No, not a stick," Bigger mentally corrected.

A wand. Though bent and gnarled, there was little doubt it was meant to channel power.

"Come!" Eanna demanded. "There is no time!"

Looking over his shoulder, Bigger entered the screened room. Water sloshed from the tub as Eanna stood, leaned across the side and grabbed his hand. Yanking him forward, she brought his attention squarely back to her. The robe hung from a hook on one of the four-by-four posts that framed the room. She stood naked, droplets clinging to her skin, staring at him expectantly, her grip tight on his wrist. Bigger stared back, his pulse increasingly loud in his ears.

"Yes?" she inquired.

He answered, "Yes," but it was mindless.

"He finds me by my thoughts of him!"

She shook his arm impatiently.

"He knows he is close!"

"Yes," Bigger thought. She had said something like that the night before.

"MacGregor!" she barked. "You must distract me. Your life depends on it!"

Bigger's gaze dropped from the fire in her eyes to her nipples, invitingly erect. Droplets hung from each, flashing when sudden lightning struck near the road.

"What?" he asked.

Bigger shivered alert.

"Distract...?"

Eanna did not wait. Yanking the waist of his sweat pants to his knees, she pulled, meaning to topple him into the tub. He resisted, hopping from one leg to the other to free himself from the garment. Finally, answering her insistent grip, he splashed naked into the water.

She molded to him. Her hand behind his neck drew him to a kiss. Before he lost himself on her lips, a glow at the back of the enclosure caught Bigger's eye.

"What's that light?" he asked, trying to pull free to investigate. "There shouldn't be anything—"

"Leave that alone!" she ordered. "Pay attention."

"But," he objected, "If there's a short where it can splash, or if the conduit—"

"There is nothing wrong with the conduit."

She turned him around with surprising force, and pressed him to the back rim of the tub.

"As a matter of fact," her eyebrow flicked, "Everything is exactly right with the conduit. Sit."

Bigger sat. She had positioned him on a bench formed along the rear of the tub, just below the water's surface. Vertical behind him was a two-inch diameter pipe enclosing the power lines for the tub's machinery. Like so much else about the house, its was a legacy installation from previous owners, one of a list of modifications he intended to redo when time and other priorities allowed. A layer of polymer waterproofing had been an interim fix that eased his concern about electrocution and, happily, gave the conduit a decorative appearance. Eanna guided his hands behind his back one at a time and placed them on the pipe.

Her eyes glittered as she instructed, "Do not let go."

Fortunately the tub was shaped so that its rim formed a back to the bench. He was able to lean against it comfortably, at least for a time. Whether or not this remained so depended on how long she wanted him to hold the conduit. He started to ask, but she placed a finger across his mouth.

"Do not talk."

Lightning struck again, this time by the fence. Bigger jumped at the flash and boom, throwing his hands wide. In one motion, Eanna thrust herself between his legs and seized his wrists. Wrestling his hands to the conduit, she brought her face to his. An inch, less, separated their noses. Her expression hardened.

Voice unyielding, she ordered, "Do...not...move."

He started to object, but her finger went to his lips.

"If you let go of that pipe, or if you say a word, I shall leave you to the consequences. Do...not...move."

The storm hit. A flood dropped from heaven. Wind lashed chill mist through the wire screen that was their shield. Eanna ignored the onslaught. She sank to her knees, her mouth slowly forming a theatrical pout. His eyes flicked away when the wind brought sounds of the feral pack, but her hands grasped the soft form of his penis and drove out thought. She rolled his quickening erection between her palms.

"Now."

She conceded the ghost of a smile to his gasp.

"This time you will respect the queen of heaven."

Bigger opened his mouth like he might say something, but Eanna opened hers and enfolded the crown of his cock between her lips. The world went silent. The whole of Bigger's existence collapsed to the feel of her tongue on his flesh. Her hands played its tightening length, seeming to hold him suspended. Only his grip on the conduit tied him to the familiar.

She closed her lips lightly, and, for a heartbeat, held motionless. Almost imperceptibly, she began to work her jaw, drawing him cell by cell deeper into warm and wet. Her caressing tongue and the heat of her mouth kept him taut, pleasure colored with an edge of pain.

Bigger floated submerged in a well of silence. His awareness shrank to the actions of her hands and lips, her deft tongue, and suction from the slow, fluffing bellows of her cheeks. The rest of his being felt nothing, experienced nothing. There was only the burgeoning charge of her touch.

Eanna allowed her teeth to scrape the fleshy cap between them, firing a spasm of panic through Bigger that churned the tub. When he jumped, she tightened her lips to his cock and began to suck, gently, without moving her head. Her thumbs slid back and forth along the bottom of his shaft, her fingers resting laced along the top. Working her cheeks, she slowly drew and relaxed, repeating the action without hurry, repeating it again.

A quiver ran through his body. His breathing grew labored and deep. In small reciprocations, she moved her head, sliding an inch of him in and out of her mouth. One of her hands drifted to rest on his belly. The edge of her palm clocked his accelerating heart, rising and falling with the heaving of his chest. She allowed herself a twitch of smile, which caused her teeth to close infinitesimally. Bigger registered the tiny movement with a gasp.

Adrift in a parallel state, he was not aware of the raggedness of his breathing, but its shushing regularity turned a key in his perception. Muffled, but moment by moment gaining volume, gaining clarity, a pounding boom engulfed him. Like a kettledrum racing from a distance, the beat rode a tearing wheeze in the soundtrack to his trance. The sound dismayed him only a moment, as he knew it from the previous night. The throb of his heart was familiar; so was the gale of his breath.

Eanna bobbed faster, locking to his pulse. With each successive stroke she pushed more of him into her mouth. She willed not to gag, her entire upper body straining with a force that splashed over the far side of the tub. Abruptly, she slapped both hands to the cheeks of his ass and hauled him forward, struggling to open for his entire length. Drawn like a bow, Bigger churned the water spastically. Eanna pressed steadily, but her throat would not accept him.

She relaxed, holding him gently with her front teeth, panting for breath before starting again. Pulling a hand forward, Eanna circled his penis with her thumb and forefinger. Alternately, she squeezed and rolled, then she plunged her mouth again, straining without success to take his flesh into her throat. Bigger planted his heels at the small of her back. Ragged gasps tore from his lungs.

The stimulation of her mouth erased the rest of his world. He kicked involuntarily, unaware, and struck only water, but the force of the spasm threw Eanna off and under the surface.

She shot up flailing and choking. Wide-eyed, Bigger looked on, hands still locked, as by a spell, to the conduit.

Without warning, teeth rushed from every side.

Gigantic teeth crashed upon them like they had been sucked into a chewing mouth. Tiny teeth champed at them, ravening. Thousands of teeth, all sizes but somehow all the same, came like biting hail.

Bigger bucked with pain as the choppers tore at them, but Eanna spat to clear her airway and placed a palm flat above his heart to keep him in place. Dropping upon him, she drew new life into his briefly flagging erection with her mouth and tongue. The teeth pressed ever tighter upon them.

Eanna became two. So it looked to him. Only thus could he constitute what was happening. Her mouth and hand remained upon him, her head moving rhythmically up and down. She continued to kneel before him, continued to hold him thrall with her mouth, even as she, another she, a greater she, towering, rose up. Thrusting wide her hands, she shoved away the harrowing teeth, and then twisted, contracting, winding up.

Teeth swarmed her, chomping, gnashing, a biting hunger that tore hunks of her flesh and oozed blood from countless wounds. With a furious shout, Eanna the Titan burst into motion, her arms windmilling to claw space free from the invasion.

Her bites healed in an instant. The ichor that had dripped from them absorbed back through her skin.

Her frenzied counter sped up, but took on nuance. Wild flailing became a dance, a kinetic flow of arms and legs pushing out, creating a sphere impervious to attack. In the center, her human-sized self still rhythmically sucked a human-sized member.

Gradually, a glow emerged from the woman crouched between his legs, first dimly limning Bigger's features, then throwing them, at last, into sharp relief. Panting under her assiduous touch, he hardly noticed her growing brilliance, even when it sparkled through the lashes of his heavy-lidded eyes. He had sensed the glow behind the conduit. He sensed her luminosity too bright to look upon. He did not care.

Lightning blasted from the air around their heads, coming from nowhere. Eanna collapsed into a single woman thrown across his leg, glow extinguished. Stunned by the concussion, Bigger was able to look on but unable to resist as the teeth came at them. He swung his head side to side to avoid incisors tearing his face.

Dentition of a thousand mouths swarmed Eanna, ripping away her flesh in strips. She writhed as her skin was torn from the muscle beneath, and convulsed when the teeth shredded the raw meat from her bones.

Some part of Bigger knew this while it happened, though shock and pain swamped any chance he would interfere. The first of the teeth had swarmed the woman, but there was torment enough for both of them. Bigger had only an instant to see Eanna shredded to gobbets before he, too, was attacked.

The pain was beyond anything he could have imagined. Blood ran, swelling from some bites, jetting from others. He seemed frozen in hurt, his arms no less locked behind him than if bound. Teeth ripping flesh from his body, he thrashed, trying to protect his face, trying to protect his eyes.

Even under assault he saw, clearly, the crescents of meat bitten from his torso, the morsels chewed from below his eyes and, through a haze of their mingled blood, Eanna's failing quiver as she was stripped to a naked skeleton.

His agony grew tenfold when she ceased moving.

The attack redoubled and doubled again. His throat was torn away when he lifted his head to scream. Bite by rending bite, muscle was flensed from bone until it was not possible for more to be taken. Yet the torment went on. Beyond every mouthful of flesh remained another, the last shreds of tissue renewed, the last welling ooze of blood endlessly replenished. A new agony, like drowning, enveloped Bigger when the teeth found his organs and devoured his lungs. Time snapped to a halt. Nothing remained of him but excruciation.

Then a jagged band of gore reappeared on his bone in a slash of relief, heightening the torment to the rest of him. Another slash brought back more blood, more tissue, and with it a flash of vision.

A flicker of sight, impossible in his collapse, lit the dogs in the yard, battling the man with too many teeth. The villain danced nimbly. Jerking, leaping, he spun to escape them, but the snapping jaws of Belle and Toro tore as ruthlessly as the disembodied teeth overrunning the hot tub. Belle attached herself to the man's side; Toro lunged repeatedly for his throat, tearing at hands and arms as the intruder parried. Lightning struck beyond the fence, again and again, hundreds of times, with deafening blasts of thunder.

Bigger was whole again in an instant. The thousands of teeth turned to sparkling powder, and the sparkles winked out. Eanna spasmed, her restored limbs striking stiff in four directions to burst the walls of the tub. Strength flowed into woman and man as the water drained away. With open mouth, Eanna fell like an engine upon Bigger's renewed erection. She paused once to try forcing the head into her throat, but could not, and went again to bobbing violently up and down. She slid a hand beneath his balls, her middle finger finding and pressing into his anus. As she worked the stiff length of him with her mouth, she paced the stroke of her thumb against the skin taut over the gland at the join of his legs.

Pulling back until his cock spanned the gap between them, only the cap held in the loose purse of her lips,

Eanna shrugged his legs from her shoulders and started again to rise and fall with her whole body. Her mouth worked the head and upper stretch of his erection as her hand kneaded below. Her other hand slid between his legs to cup his balls. She kept her finger shoved in his ass. Her thumb tapped lightly against the tender flesh behind his scrotum.

A jolt went through him. Eanna plunged again as he lurched, trying anew to open her throat. Panting, Bigger went completely rigid when she tried without success to jam his meat through the balk of her reflexes. Letting go of his balls, she grabbed one of his nipples and rolled it, not too soft, not too hard, between fingertip and thumb. Their motion reflected her other hand, rocking below, manipulating within and without.

She pulled back on his shaft to suck hard, working her cheeks until the first convulsion of his orgasm. Curling the finger in his butt, and pushing from outside with her thumb, she jumped up, releasing his nipple to seize his chin. Eanna pulled herself forward and exhaled into his raling mouth. He came in a ropy spew onto her breasts.

The climax telegraphed through him, making him buck and kick. Hollow thuds from his blows rebounded off the breached walls of the tub. Bigger collapsed into himself as the last, spent drops of semen squirted in a weak arc from his already shrinking cock. For an instant, he saw her face swim toward him, the strange glow of the secret object behind the tub reflected in her eyes. His own silhouette overlaid her pupils. For that one instant only, he thought. Then she ceased blowing into his mouth and moved almost to a kiss. Before their lips touched, she began to inhale. Awareness of the cramping ache in his shoulders and arms came home like a blow. He lost his grip on the conduit. She suctioned away his breath as he fell back against the pipe and away from consciousness. Down, down and down, he tumbled into dark.

**III**

Again, Bigger awoke alone. On his bed, he sprawled atop the covers.

Fleeting irritation that Eanna was not there gave way to gurgling from his belly. He had eaten nothing since she had walked up his driveway. The instant he moved, he knew he was famished. At the same time, he discovered his whole body felt battered. Slowly, diagnostically, he stretched as he dressed. Every muscle and joint resisted.

Bigger exited the house pulling overalls straps onto his shoulders, and crossed the yard to release the chickens. Birds pecking at a scatter of scratch, he went through nest boxes collecting eggs. As he turned back to the kitchen with hands full, a pedal van drove through the gate.

Though he had come of age just as the old United States had fragmented, Bigger still remembered the crippled postal service and private delivery companies of that dead formation. He had doubts about follow-on solutions in some of the other successor states, but the agency that served the fledgling republic in which he now found himself citizen was effective and reliable. As they conveyed the majority of his raw materials, he had reason to know.

Changing course to intercept the vehicle, he expected not the usual driver of his route, but a fill-in who had made the past few deliveries. Instead, when the van came to a stop, a woman stepped from the driver's cockpit, her face impishly alight.

"Quella!" Bigger exclaimed, hurrying with arms wide to sweep her into a hug

53

He squeezed her hard, framing her face with eggs and fingers.

"Willie delivered the last two times, and he doesn't talk. I was getting worried."

He reddened.

"I tried to call, but the signal kept failing."

Quella showed him the dead screen of her phone, and slid it back into a pocket.

"Every time I turn it on, it shuts off. Charge is good, so I don't know."

She tickled his rib.

"You can always write me a letter, lover boy. Willie doesn't say much, but he never misses a delivery."

She sobered, but only a little.

"I've been under the weather, BUT...," grinning, she gave his rib another poke, "Not enough to burden the odd casual friend!"

Though slight, her stress on the word "casual" was pregnant. Laughing, she missed him jerk as if pushed, and also his second reaction, when the sense of what she said struck home. Quella went on, carried by her obvious pleasure at seeing him.

"I consulted that funny little aunt of yours, by the way. Ekaterina? Yeah. Her concoctions won't win any taste awards, but they work better than what they compound at the pharmacy."

Pouting theatrically, she thrust out her lower lip.

"Sorry, Mac. No whoopee for at least another week."

This hung between them a fractional instant. She held up a plastic basket.

"Here's a quart of strawberries to tide you over."

"Quella!"

Worry made his voice break.

"Are you all right?"

Eyes narrow, he searched her face.

"I mean really all right."

Bigger started to reach, intending to touch her cheek, but stopped at sight of the eggs in his hand.

"Are you okay?"

He brushed her shoulder with the back of his wrist.

"Hey!"

Cautiously, to avoid dislodging eggs, she slipped her hand over his.

"After the federal collapse, we got a real union down here in the hidden lands. The contract guarantees I won't ever pedal this thing if I'm not certifiably sound."

Again, she lifted the basket.

"Strawberries? They're heirloom. Symbiont free. Grew 'em myself."

"Strawberries!"

Bigger shook his head, as if disbelieving his luck.

"Wonderful!"

He made a mental inventory of the state of the house, and displayed his egg-filled hands before her.

"I was on the way to breakfast. Have time for scrambled eggs and fruit?"

"Nope."

She turned toward the van.

"I rolled out here to the far point first. It's going to take all day to work back to the depot. Let me unload this ton of stuff you're getting, and then it's *besos, abrazos y hasta luego, querido*. I gotta scram."

He ran his eggs inside while she pulled an assortment of cartons from the van. Planting a peck on his cheek, she hopped into the driver's seat, whipped through a tight U, shifted gears and rolled out the gate. The vehicle rocked to the churn of her legs. Bigger watched her down the drive, but turned away before she was out of sight. He began shifting his deliveries into the work bays.

Sorting the materials as he carried them in, he scanned UPCs with his tablet and stowed goods to shelves or cabinets as appropriate. Spools of plant-derived polymer fiber, spools of glass fiber, polymer binder in powder form, meter-long rods of various kinds of steel, similar rods of aluminum and brass, and three huge spools of all-purpose carbon nanotube received ticks on his checklist. Various resins and paints had not arrived, but were still in the expected delivery window. He lacked for nothing this day's work would require. Bigger headed inside to fresh eggs and strawberries.

Seated at his breakfast, he was surprised by a physical memory of holding Quella, strong and sturdy, in his arms. His flush of guilt was tagged by the shorthand of a single name. Eanna. He had said nothing about the latter to the former.

There had not been time. Much of what he might have confessed had been beyond his control. Excuses popped to mind unbeckoned. It did not matter. His attention strayed to the meal on his plate. Despite an effort to lay out practical steps for the morning, he could not let go of the thought of a conversation that would only grow more difficult with delay.

In truth, mundane organizing didn't stand a chance. With one imperative pressing as he chewed his eggs, Bigger also recalled the feel of another body. As muscle and skin remembered Quella, so they remembered his lover of the previous nights. The memories tingled with a physical charge not entirely pleasant. The wonderful parts washed through him. The bad parts brought him somewhere near critical mind.

How was he to question a woman whose current whereabouts were unknown?

What concerned him was not Eanna's absence or presence, but questions he had not asked and subjects they had not broached.

With great force, as though to make up for not having wondered before, he mentally framed, "Who is this woman from nowhere demanding sex?"

The question roiled his curiosity as he tried to fix it in mind for later, but almost without notice, it morphed into, "What does she have to do with those teeth?"

Absently biting a strawberry, he wondered what this exotic stranger had brought upon his home.

From where he sat at the table he could see across the main room and through the screen door to Belle and Toro relaxed but alert on the porch.

"Why," he asked himself, "do the dogs like her?"

Struck by a single detail remembered from two different places, he stopped chewing and swallowed to ask, "What was that strange blue light?"

Questions cluttered his mind as he walked back to the bay. Standing before Eanna's car, he did not really see it at first, though he stared at the driver's hatch and pondered the absent driver. Finally, the car came into focus at the core of another question: what was the origin of this vehicle? What builder would have created this machine but left no obvious maker's mark? With no more way to answer that question than any of his others, he turned to the work at hand.

Morning passed as Bigger fabricated a section of ceramic barrel to replace the failed original. While the part cured, he ground the spur from the steel finger that would ride within the newly-minted slot. They snugged well in a test fit, and he broke for lunch satisfied with his progress. There was chicken soup to reheat. And there were strawberries.

Coming to the table with his lunch, he noticed that the lid of Eanna's wooden chest was not tightly closed. It flipped open with the flick of a finger, its hinges silent and smooth. A dim blue glow from the contents contrasted starkly with the box's obvious age. Neat ranks and files of plastic-capped vials, dozens of them, almost filled the interior. Two spots were empty. Inspection showed the vials bore minimal labeling, no more than a UPC and the designation, "Entheoclone 36." The term nagged at him, almost but not quite meaningful.

"Inner god copy," he guessed from its parts. "Or something like that. But why 36?"

Retrieving his notebook, he tapped in a search that returned a welter of hits from the far fringe.

Most discussion was on the proliferating forums of neo-Learyites or one of the reformed wings of the Castanedians. A hundred or so links down the list, he found an academic paper that was more than tripper fantasy. Describing Entheoclone 36 as a compound undergoing trial in extreme psychiatric interventions, the report admitted that neither its chemistry nor its action was "well understood." The drug absorbed readily through the skin, and usual delivery was by transdermal patch. Some researchers preferred it as a microcomponent of an inhaled cocktail.

A property described by nearly all trial subjects was that people taking the drug in groups appeared to share hallucinations. Participants maintained that they entered a common alternate reality.

The paper stated, "When multiple users dose in close proximity, part of the expressive effect is an illusion that all users experience congruent distortions of consensus reality."

The authors noted that debate was heated between those who argued that hallucinations actually were shared and those of the authors' own camp who maintained that this was unsubstantiated and anecdotal.

A lengthy footnote related to this property implicated the drug in increasing numbers of recreational suicides. In a typical scenario compiled from police reports and grand jury proceedings, those choosing to die—the "death-marked"—surrounded themselves with a cohort of from one to many. The death-marked would each take a deliberate overdose, a quantity sufficient to kill by ecstatic dissolution of the self. Those in the cohort would take single doses in order to participate in the "mortgasm" of the dissolving self—usually without sharing the actual death. Both the game and the drug involved were known popularly as "Trip Out."

Global police cartels were convinced Entheoclone 36 and Trip Out were the same. Again, there were dissenters. A well-argued paper based on cloud sampling maintained that Trip Out was actually the chemically distinct Entheoclone 23b. Unfortunately, all the citations were dead links, and Bigger found no further mention of any Entheoclone other than 36. Most of that was unhelpful. One notice, however, on a bulletin board associated with the flying encyclopedia of the Black Arts Collective, sourced vials filled with blue-glowing dermal patches to classified labs in the Lubbock Free State. By pedal car, the Lubbock Free State was a day's hard drive from where Bigger sat.

Unsure if he had been enlightened, Bigger closed the box, leaving the lid ajar as he had found it.

***

Walking back from the house to the shop, he stumbled and nearly fell on the little red hen, scurrying underfoot to stay inside his stride.

He stopped to demand of her, "What are you doing?"

The hen clucked softly, and cocked her head. She stretched her neck to peer vaguely into the distance. When Bigger stepped deliberately over the bird to start again for the shop, she hurried to travel with him.

As he moved around the bay preparing to work, the little hen settled atop a toolbox, turning her head in nervous jerks to follow his activity. After a few moments, however, she hopped down and trotted purposefully out. Bigger smiled and shook his head without consciously noticing the bird. His thoughts, instead, churned around Eanna. There were huge gaps in what he could explain about events since her arrival. When she returned, he resolved, they would sit and talk.

Afternoon wore away as Bigger rebuilt the drive train of his visitor's car. Imagined fragments of the conversation he anticipated having with her played through his thoughts while his hands explored, evaluated and memorized the specifics of her vehicle. Most of its lines were quite elegant, but here and there the designer in him would note a curve that could be refined for greater efficiency, or a stress point that could be more robust. His hands worked knowing these exceptions were quibbles, really, almost mute acknowledgements of skill shared with an unknown artisan.

***

In golden light of approaching evening, Bigger rolled out the reassembled pedal car for a test drive. More than half the moon already showed pink above the eastern hills. When he reached the end of the driveway, he saw Eanna on his bicycle coasting down the road from the hill, and stopped to wait. She put her feet down as she skidded up beside him. Bigger stepped from the vehicle and took hold of the bike, indicating the open driver's sling with a nod.

"Better if you do this and tell me it's right than for me to try guessing what will make you happy."

Her eyes narrowed with suspicion of a double meaning, but she slid into the car and started up the lane. Bigger held the bicycle and watched. Distant thunder drew his attention west. Another storm was billowing up to swallow the sun standing huge and red on the horizon. He turned to find Eanna paused, also watching the sky. She glanced at him. Leaning into the pedals, she popped the transmission, and the car lurched forward. When she neared, Bigger directed her down the drive toward his yard. Eanna rolled through the gate to a stop.

"Finally!" She exclaimed as Bigger coasted in behind her on the bike.

He gave her a curious look. She ignored him while she beamed at the sign on his shop, his foraging chickens, and the few tarp-covered vehicles still tied down in the yard.

"Finally?"

His voice rose with the question.

"Finally I have arrived at your compound as I set out for it. By car."

Bigger's mouth twitched at this, but he commented only, "You'll get a smoother start if you pump the pedals a few times before engaging the transmission. That'll charge the flywheels enough to power out of the stop."

Eanna arched a brow. Her lips curled.

"And if I pump you, Mr. MacGregor?"

He had not thought about how to open their necessary talk, but here it was. Bigger scowled.

"How about I pump you?"

Before she could react, he added, "For answers. Sitting at a table."

He looked her up and down.

"Across from each other."

She glanced at the sky and began, "The old one—"

He threw his hands in the air and strode past her toward the house. In the middle of the yard, he spun and took a step back. Eanna faced him, her head framed by the rising moon. The Rose Moon. Its face shone with a namesake blush, a glow refracted off the storm by the setting sun.

"The old one," Bigger repeated. "What if tonight we keep the bogey man away with a conversation?"

"To speak of him—" she began, but he slashed the air with his hand.

"No!"

Bigger shook his head and started again for the house.

"Not him. I do not want to talk about him."

Mounting the steps, he tossed back, "The only topic that concerns me is you."

The little red wandering hen waited on the porch beside the door. When Bigger rattled the screen, the dogs rose from the shade under the eaves of the repair bay and loped toward the house. The hen darted inside as soon as the door opened, but the dogs, arriving before Eanna, waited beside Bigger. She walked without hurry, climbed the steps, and strode across the porch. Bigger held the door with one hand, inviting the dogs inside with a sweep of the other. Toro acknowledged him with a look, but then flopped down on the porch. Belle moved to a point on the other side of the door, circled it three times, and lowered herself to the decking. Bigger shrugged and passed in.

Sounds of Eanna already in the shower reached him as he closed the door. He went to the kitchen. By the time she emerged from the bathroom combing out wet hair, he had dinner underway. Eanna glided to a stop beside a bowl of lettuce Bigger had plucked from his window boxes. Mixing hard-boiled egg with onions and mustard, he smiled, and jutted his chin at the fresh greens.

"How about adding imagination to that salad?"

"Do I look like a serving girl?" she snapped.

Bigger froze, staring at her.

"My mistake," he said at last, and shifted the bowl away from where she stood. "I meant no offense."

She climbed onto a kitchen stool, sniffing in the direction of the lettuce.

"What kind of food is this bowl of leaves?" she demanded. "What is wrong with bread and mutton?"

Making a face, Bigger sighed. There were explanations he had tired of making long ago.

"That's just not my regular diet."

He resumed mashing eggs.

"Had I known you were coming, I'd have laid in vast stores of mutton and bread. As it stands, I can only offer what I have. If it will make you happy, I'll kill a chicken."

She opened her mouth to respond, but was interrupted by a clap of thunder that engulfed the house. Eanna's eyes grew large.

She reached for Bigger, exclaiming, "Hurry! You must distract me...."

Bigger held up a hand and said, "Not yet."

She looked shocked.

Bigger repeated, "Not yet."

She stared.

"First, we eat," he told her. "And talk."

"Talk?" she asked.

"Yes," he insisted. "No offense, but there are things I need to know, and there doesn't seem much chance you'll stick around in the morning."

"Only while the moon is in the sky."

"Only while...," he began to parrot, but stopped himself. "I guess that means talk fast."

She stared at him, fidgeting. Lightning struck close, but neither of them jumped or looked away. Bigger nodded.

"Right," he said at last, but then scratched his head, unsure now that he had her attention.

Casting for a way in, he asked, "Who built your car?"

She hesitated before answering.

"No one you have heard of. What does it matter?"

His whole body tensed with dissatisfaction at this answer. Bigger willed the strain from his muscles.

"There's a question of possible patent violations," he informed her. Levelly, he added, "My patents."

Eanna chewed her lip, defensive for the first time since her arrival. She crossed her arms over her chest, and uncrossed them.

At last, she said flatly, "The builder is not subject to such constraints."

"Okay."

He took her hand and drew her resisting to the couch.

"You're going to have to explain that one. And dinner will have to wait until you convince me."

They sat, Bigger with a leg up on the cushion so that he faced her. Eanna folded forward, giving him her profile, refused to meet his eye. She shifted nervously. He waited, but she showed no sign of opening up. When the silence stretched on, he punctured it abruptly.

"Well?"

Her chest heaved, as if she sighed, but her expression was grim. Bigger was on the verge of another prompt when she began to speak.

"If you assume that your designs influenced the construction of my car, you are correct. The...community ...to which I belong has an interest in your innovations. We have followed your work for some time. I was impressed by the way you improved your father's designs without calling his attention to the fact, but it was that collapsible aircraft that drew notice by our full council—"

"The pedal plane?" he broke in, astonished. "I made that when I was twelve!"

She gave him a searching look.

"Do you really not know me?" she asked.

Bigger stared at her, eyes wide, willing himself to see through the mystery without knowing what he was supposed to see.

"No..., I...."

He looked harder, but then shook his head.

"For a moment you reminded me of someone. Your expression, but…," he trailed off.

"But you do not think I am that person."

She stated it as fact. Bigger laughed.

"No, not unless you used to be blonde, blue-eyed and six inches taller."

Eanna smiled.

"And, too, with wider hips and larger breasts?"

Upon these words, she struck a posture of rapt listening he found eerily familiar. Puzzled by a memory that did not fit this face, or this body, he gazed at Eanna, his thoughts a scatter. She listened intently to his almost silent breath. There was the sound of random drops hitting windowpanes.

Finally, he ventured, "You knew Rebecca?"

The pause before she answered grew long.

"Knew is an interesting word. It suggests the knowing has closed and is past."

Falling back against the couch, she crossed her arms over her chest and set her mouth as though she would say no more. Bigger sat taut, a spring in check.

"Are you from the hospital?" he blurted. "No, let me rephrase that. Do you work for the hospital, or did you escape from it? Is that where you got the drugs?"

Fire in her eyes, Eanna leapt up.

"You understand nothing!" she shouted.

"That's right!" he countered without rising. "That's exactly right! I understand nothing. That's why you're going to explain it to me, because I do not understand."

His voice rose as he went on.

"Not about why you're here, not about that box of drugs, or the guy with the teeth, or the theft of my designs. And, now, especially, I do not understand what you have to do with Rebecca!"

As if to underscore his frustration, lightning struck close, near the road. They both jumped. Eanna clenched, opened and reclenched her fists.

"You MUST act!" she commanded. "There is no time!"

"Sit!" Bigger snapped.

He stopped, and brought himself under control.

More gently, he said, "Please sit down."

When she did not, his voice tightened.

"I mean it. I'm not moving from this couch until I know what's going on."

Eanna glowered.

Unyielding, he stared back.

"Start with something easy," he said at last. "Like the drug you slipped me the past two nights. What about that?"

Eanna made no attempt to deny the accusation, bristling instead.

"You have no business—"

He cut her off with an upraised hand.

"I looked. You left the box half-opened on the table and I looked. Take that as fact and move on, okay? My question is, why have you brought a lifetime's supply of a powerful, probably illegal entheogen into my home? And while you're at it, why did you dose me without my consent?"

She looked set for another outburst, her mouth fidgeting and her eyes flashing. When she continued, however, she was almost subdued.

"You really understand nothing."

He started to react, but she slashed the air with her hand and ordered, "Do not interrupt!"

Her eyes closed and she seemed to struggle.

"I am trying to tell you."

Lightning struck again, closer. The thunderclap rattled the structure. Before the walls stopped trembling, rain began to pelt down. Eanna closed her eyes and muttered, her voice barely loud enough for Bigger to tell she again spoke in the guttural tongue he had heard before. The sound of the rain became muted, and the thunder, which continued, seemed to draw away from them. Bigger made as if to say something, but Eanna lifted a palm to still him. When she started speaking, it was so softly that he had to lean forward to hear.

"You must look into your heart to know what I say is truth. You must look into your heart to believe you have known me before this."

She gazed at him intensely. Bigger felt recognition stir, like a hint of memory. He started to name the inkling, but stopped, overcome by confusion. Eanna nodded, and reached to smooth his brow. Her tone was confessional.

"I was not prepared for the violence of your priests when I entered your Rebecca."

The statement struck like a blow.

"*Entered*...Rebecca?" he repeated. "What...?"

"I should not have been surprised," she confided. "Their injections had almost driven me from the girl, Emilia, before Rebecca arrived. You remember Emilia? By the time I transfered to Rebecca, poor Emilia was so damaged by the injections that she was no more than an empty vessel. When I was no longer there to move her, there was no longer an Emilia to fill the shell. The priests were relentless."

"The girl."

Bigger snapped his fingers.

"The first girl, with dementia. Rebecca's roommate. That's who you mean?"

"Dementia!" Eanna spat. "A word! The priests murdered her. They sought to drive me out with no other suitable host. All they did was kill the girl. They killed her while I sat within the vessel. When I left, there was only shell, even if it breathed."

She shook her head, as though dismayed by her own words. Bigger waited for her to go on, but, she sat unresponsive, musing. The house creaked and moaned, moved by silent winds. At last, she continued.

"These priests and their chemicals. Acolytes of chemicals, and they do not even know what they have. Poisons and dust and shadows of power. When something genuine, something true, comes into their hands, they tremble in fear and lock it away. The keys are in their hands, but still they turn to poisons, or worse, the bolts of the old one!"

Lightning struck again, punctuating her words. The flash of light and sound of thunder were still muted, though close enough that blue light threw the room into relief. A ghost of the thunderclap reached them. Anger passed over Eanna's face.

"It is not a simple thing, holding him at bay!" she boasted. "Your life is in play. If he comes through the barrier, you will not be spared."

"He who?"

Bigger's temper matched hers.

"If 'he who' comes through the barrier? Quit trying to scare me with a bogeyman! You're going to talk to me!"

"Do you not remember last night?" she coaxed.

"Last night!" he exploded. "I'm onto your game, Eanna! I know about the drugs, and I know you're up to something. What I don't know is what that may be or why you're here. Why me?"

"Why you?" she shouted back. "I do not know why you! You opened the chest and saw what you expected to see. You know nothing! Drugs!"

She raked the air with her nails.

"Your priests talk of drugs even as they deny the worlds to which they gain access! Once, you were different from them. Once you were a man apart, a man I respected. Who are you now? I do not know! Why you? I guess because I am sentimental for a time when you were extraordinary!"

She flopped hard against the back of the couch, sprawling with a finality that suggested she had washed her hands of the topic. The house creaked loudly into the silence between them. From outside came thunder, still muted by whatever strange filter made their conversation possible.

Bigger leapt to his feet and began to pace, his head bobbing as he sussed her words.

"Once I was different, you said."

He stopped, letting his stare draw her eyes.

"When? Yesterday? Some other time, before we met?"

He took another step, but turned back to her.

"Why, exactly, are you here? Why did you come...,"

With both hands, he indicated where he stood.

"Here?"

Eanna's expression softened. She seemed, for an instant, on the verge of growing misty. Her voice, when she answered, slipped into the space between them, quiet with regret.

"Bigger MacGregor, you really do not know me? This is what tells me that you understand nothing."

Bigger groaned in frustration.

"So you tell me."

He looked away from her, watching muted rain sheet down the outside of the window. Absently, he crossed the room and cranked the shutters closed.

Without turning back toward her, he went on, "Enlighten me. Explain what I don't understand. If you don't want to start with why you are here—or why me—start with your lifetime supply of a drug so new there aren't even any obvious laws against it."

He moved to crank the shutters on the next window.

"The drug you have shown such willingness to give me without so much as a by-your-leave."

Eanna rose and went to the window beyond the dining table to crank the shutter.

"You are wise to close the house," she observed, raising her voice more than necessary.

"Whatever excuse at hand," he commented, possibly to himself.

Her face clouded, but she stifled an urge to lash out.

"Your priests think the same about the blue ichor."

She turned halfway toward him, her hand still on the shutter crank.

"They think it a drug. All the time they discuss its chemistry, and think they discuss something. Always, they try to find out who makes this, but it is not made like they hope to find. It is not a drug; it is a key. It is a key, and it comes from beyond the gate that it opens."

Bigger laughed out loud. Eanna's explanation angered him. In his anger, he found it amusing.

"Oh, the *gate*."

He almost choked on the word.

"It's obvious you spent time around Rebecca when her world was collapsing. The only thing she would talk about the last time she recognized me at all was trying to find a key to the inner gate."

"MacGregor!" Eanna cried, "That was me!"

Quickly, she added, "Wait! Wait while I do this! We must be ready!"

Leaving Bigger to stew or follow, she raced from room to room, closing shutters on windows. After a moment, he moved to secure those on his end of the house. They returned to the living room at the same time, Bigger half-angry and Eanna breathless. He turned on a lamp to drive back the gloom that had deepened during their exertions. She stood waiting beside the couch until he joined her. She gestured for him to sit with her.

"I tell you again, that was me."

She pulled up her legs and tucked them beneath her, pressing her spine into the angle where the couch's back met its arm. Bigger said nothing, and Eanna did not wait to see if he would.

"I first transferred to Rebecca as soon as she was admitted. Remaining with Emilia when the priests blasted her head with thunderbolts, I could protect her somewhat, but it was such a drain on me, and I could do less against their injections. In the beginning, I waited with Rebecca while the priests destroyed Emilia, trying to erase me. Once your Rebecca overcame her fear of me, she was a more suitable vehicle than the girl, and I began to habituate to her as Emilia's spirit died."

He watched her face change again as she realized she had to admit something she would rather not. This time, her hesitation was an instant.

"Unfortunately, I grew careless, and the priests realized that I was sometimes active through your lover. They escalated their assaults on her, and began to strike her with thunderbolts. The crime repeated. They blasted the soul from your woman and poisoned her body. You witnessed her collapse. Those times when she seemed to know you...."

Eanna hesitated.

"That was me."

She actually swallowed hard before telling him, "Rebecca was lost through the gate long before she died."

"Oh, really?" Bigger snarled. "All those months of the skipping slide into dementia, it was you that showed up for the lucid visits? You? I don't know whether to laugh or puke! And just who, exactly, are you, Ms. High-and-Mighty of the key to the gate?"

Eanna stirred.

"This being that you see, that you touch, is an avatar! Through this mouth speaks the great queen of heaven and earth. I am here trying to share knowledge freed from the trove of the old one. That is why I have come to this plane. That is why I have come to this house. That is why I have come to you!"

"I see."

Seething, Bigger fought to calm himself.

"That's rich. 'Freed from the trove of the old one.' You stole some guy's drugs, right? You stole a boutique dealer's stash, and led him straight to this isolated spot. Thank you. Thank you very much."

A huge crash, unmuffled, startled them both. Bigger rushed from the house. A cottonwood outside the fence had fallen onto the shop building, crushing one end of the structure and smashing the chicken coop. As Bigger bounded from the porch, dogs of the feral pack raced up the fallen trunk and into the yard.

From the head of the steps, Eanna shouted, "He has pierced the circle!"

The first dogs through began killing chickens in a frenzy.

Toro exploded from the house, hitting the screen door so hard that it slammed against the wall. Belle came sailing behind in a leap that carried her over Toro and the steps to land in full forward charge. Bigger's dogs hit the intruders in a murderous dance.

He ran barehanded to defend his chickens, but Eanna screamed, "MacGregor!"

He turned just in time to catch a walking stick she had thrown. Whirling the staff, Bigger laid into the wild dogs. Three of the pack's leaders attacked him.

Toro and Belle fought mainly on their hind legs, spinning and twisting with savagery that tore through their foes. Within seconds, both bled from wounds. Some dogs kept killing chickens as the battle raged around them, shaking the hens and chomping panicked chicks.

Bigger felt Eanna's fingertips slap the bare skin of his neck, and knew she had placed a transdermal patch. He swept a dog off its feet with his staff, then the world transformed. The sky brightened into a swirl of colors. The invaders deformed in some way, indescribable but unquestionably ugly.

Eanna strode past him, not the woman he had faced moments before, but the giant warrior he had seen in the hot tub. She flung wide her arms, and the feral pack was scattered. They recovered quickly as the man with too many teeth appeared in the gap where the tree had collapsed the workshop.

Eanna faced off against the new threat, but Bigger was suddenly too busy with the redoubled assault of the pack to follow her duel. He swept a slobbering beast from its feet and slammed down the stick to break the back of another. The jaws of a third closed on his leg.

The pain was excruciating, like flaming venom tearing into his flesh. Slashing behind with the stick, he heard and felt bone shatter. The bite released, but Bigger was staggered. His leg threatened to collapse. Barely in time, he parried a charging mongrel, but remained upright only by jabbing the staff against the earth.

Chickens forgotten, Belle smashed into the attacking dogs to fight by his wounded side. Toro battled through the invaders, dispatching two on the way. Both his dogs bled from multiple wounds. So did most of the attackers.

The number of them astonished him. No trace he had ever found suggested the pack totaled more than a dozen.

Dead and dying, blood from several times that number mixed with the rain washing his grounds. The corpses were all sizes, ogreous, malformed, those still in the battle likewise. What Bigger could not fathom was that there were so many. Given the number killed, there should have been none left. He whirled to face movement in his peripheral vision. Like a blur unfolding, an unblooded hound came into being, new to the fight. It crouched, snarling at silent, enraged Belle.

Violence mounting, lightning struck again and again, erupting from the air to converge on giant Eanna. Dancelike, the warrior fought the lightning as an adversary, deflecting strikes with kicks and sweeping arms. Broken bolts drained into the sodden ground. Bigger turned away in time to see Toro menaced by a dog lunging from nowhere, and then found himself facing another. It rushed him.

Huge discharges exploded on all sides, drenching the battle in chaotically strobing light. Thunder concussed the air away from the struggle at its center. Gasping to breathe in the tenuous atmosphere, Bigger still managed to jam his staff between the forelegs of the beast that charged him. The creature's momentum broke when it smashed chest-first against the butt of the stick, but Bigger was thrown to the ground. Exultation howled from the pack as he struggled to get up, shielded by the whirling fury of Toro and Belle.

Trying to rise, he found a gigantic hound upon him. It pounced. Bigger thrust the stick between closing jaws and held on, foul, steaming breath blasting his face. Sharp nails drew blood when the monster stamped his belly as it grappled with the stick. Bigger's arms grew weak. His consciousness wavered. He saw swarming points of light.

Hot, sudden weight knocked the wind from his chest as the hound collapsed onto him. The creature pushed off from Bigger's sternum with a jerk, still gripping the stick. Bigger was yanked staggering to his feet. The world spun, and his wounded leg threatened to buckle. He focused on Toro pushing up from the side, teeth locked onto the windpipe of the adversary. Wrenching the stick from Bigger's grasp, the hound swung its head, flailing, raining punishing blows on Toro. Bigger half-fell, half-leapt forward, getting clipped on the chin when he tried to seize the staff. On the rebound, he grabbed it and threw himself forward, forcing the hound onto its back. Toro held fast and landed on top of the other animal, tightening his grip on its throat. Bigger landed face down inches from the battling dogs. Despite a reeling head, he had presence of mind to roll away.

"Eanna," he thought, articulating no more.

Peering through sheets of lightning, he saw she had grown to titanic height. The man with too many teeth had grown comparably, but was on the defensive. Eanna smote him with rays of light from her hands and eyes. The rays pelletized, striking the old one like beams of hail. He retaliated with lightning bolts, called down without control. Strikes blasted the air, the ground and the crushed end of the structure where the tree had fallen. None found Eanna.

Somehow, Bigger realized, she had grown again while he looked on, failing to notice. She now towered above the man with too many teeth. Her dress clung to her, drenched from the rain, and her hair bounced in tightly hanging coils as she battle-danced. The expression on her face was merciless.

Bigger watched, awed and fascinated, until he heard a roar from behind. Turning, he faced a mongrel, twice gigantic, that slashed both Belle and Toro in a single sweep, bowling them aside in its charge.

Bigger braced his stick and pointed it like a spear, but it snapped on impact. Stabbing blindly with the splintered end, he thrust into sudden resistance, and was lifted off the ground. His hands, abruptly slick with wet, slipped from the butt of the staff. The world went silent. Time slowed. The giant dog stood on its hind legs, thrashing its head side to side in slow motion, a grip's length of the broken staff protruding from its throat. Fixed on the throes of the dog, Bigger did not notice the rain had stopped until the clouds broke up, backlighting the creature's furious end.

Across an age, as Bigger raised a hand to wipe his brow, he saw that it and his arm were covered in blood. Looking down, he saw his clothing was tattered. Blood— some his own—covered much of it. A lot of the blood, in fact, was his. Time re-engaged.

Struggling not to faint, he took in the yard. No more attackers threatened. Dead and dying, they lay around him, far too many for a single pack. Each was in some indeterminate way grotesque. Their carcasses, mingled with feathers and hunks of chicken flesh, spread in a ring with Bigger at its center. All but a paltry few had fallen to Belle and Toro. His dogs. He looked for them.

Belle stood up stiffly from where she had been thrown by the giant dog, but sat back on her haunches, eyes on Bigger. Toro stood poised, looking past Bigger to a battle still raging. Vertigo pulled when Bigger turned too fast to look.

Eanna blasted her enemy with slugging rays from left and right. The man crouched, hunched in upon himself. Blow after blow pounded him smaller, more folded in. Eanna struck furiously, repeatedly. Each strike coursed through her entire body, beginning with a push in the nimble step of her feet. She smote, her beams a hammer, a ram, driving piles of solid light to batter her adversary.

Suddenly, the man recoiled, and shot skyward. A lightning bolt disappeared into the breaking clouds.

Unbelieving, Bigger shook his head, but the motion was too much. As the world spun, he slammed to the ground. Impact did not stop the falling.

The sky sped away. His head throbbed. He was dizzy, and nauseated. The falling went on for hours. Clouds diminished to tiny points that vanished into the blue.

Hands rocketed from on high to seize him. He snapped to a halt. Eanna loomed above, her lips moving in the shape of his name. Indistinct, her voice buzzed from the limit of earshot. Slowly, his hearing and vision pulled together. Eanna pressed, demanding an answer.

"MacGregor!" she shouted, "Talk to me!"
She grabbed his ear and tugged.
"MacGregor!"
He struggled visibly. Cords stood out in his neck.
"Leg," he finally managed.
"Your leg, yes!"
She fumbled for purchase to lift him.
"A demon bit you. Stay with me!"
He fought not to drift.
"I must get you inside," she told him.

His reply was a confused mumble, but he managed a weak nod. He could not, however, help raise himself from the ground. It took all the will he could muster to drift near consciousness as Eanna, no longer a giant, strained to raise him.

Heaving, she draped him onto her back, and pulled his arms around her neck. Bent under his dead weight, she plodded toward the house. Before each jerking step, she paused to check his stability. In the pauses, she talked to him, goading him to stay awake.

"MacGregor! You must not sleep! Answer me!"
Jarred by her lurching, he moaned.
"You fought well," she told him, adjusting her grip on his arms.

Even through pain and confusion, he heard the praise.
"Few survive a battle with demons."
Demons. The word raked his thoughts. Not demons. He fought dogs. Tens of dogs. It was a drug that made them seem ugly. Dogs. The correction would not form in his throat.

"I shall make a song. The tale of your deed will ring in heaven and...."
Her voice died. She stalled, jarring him when she staggered to keep her balance.
"Blast!" she cursed.
The foot of the steps to the porch seemed impossibly high. Eanna puffed hard as she gathered the strength to climb. Bigger, his head hanging over her shoulder, saw feathers attached to bloody flesh.

He labored to ask, "Chi-? Chi-ck?"

Eanna stamped a foot onto the lowest step.

"Dead!" she barked, shrugging him more firmly onto her back.

She grunted, hauled up another step, and managed, "Demons, too."

She raised him, boosting his weight with her leg.

"All of them."

Eanna concentrated on getting him onto the porch, trying to say nothing more. At the top, she stood for a moment finding her balance.

Bigger croaked, "Dogs? Belle?"

"They have wounds to lick," she answered. "You are worse. They will care for themselves."

Without warning, Eanna shifted, letting him flip to land on his back, controlling the fall so his head did not slam on the deck. She grabbed under his armpits and dragged him toward the door.

Passive as she pulled him, Bigger watched his dogs limp up the steps. Their worried eyes never left him. Belle had a long, shallow wound on the top of her muzzle. She also favored a leg. Bite wounds on Toro's chest and shoulder still oozed. Blue sky showed through a pinhole in his left ear. Trying to cluck reassurance, Bigger choked on his tongue.

From the spasm, darkness flooded. His eyes rolled up. Belle surged forward, stumbling on her injured limb but grabbing the knee of his overalls, which she began to shake. Bounding, Toro flew up the steps, barking furiously in Bigger's face.

Jerked from the faint by Eanna bouncing him on the deck, Bigger heard her shout, "MacGregor! Do not sleep!"

She heaved him through the door. He strained to stay awake, but the room spun, and he lost touch with what was happening. His sense returned as Eanna half-rolled him onto the couch when she swung his legs onto the cushions. The room spun again, then cleared. He started at the sound of Eanna ripping the leg of his overalls. An impulse to protest died without reaching his lips.

His eyes worked, but his head was no more responsive than the rest of his body. Peering down as far over the contours of his face as he was able, he watched her work.

The wound on his calf lay at the far edge of his vision. Luminous green and purple streaks spread up and down from the bite. Eanna spun and left his view, returning a moment later with her wooden chest. From the box she took a tube and shook out two dermal patches. One she stuck on Bigger's neck, the other on her own. In the rush of the drug, he saw her draw a knife, apparently from thin air, and wipe it with a cotton pad. The smell of rubbing alcohol burned his nose. Toro licked Bigger's dangling hand, distracting him the instant Eanna cut.

The knife was sharp enough that he did not feel it slice, but instantly he felt pressure ease. Pain expanded in its wake. Eanna leaned forward, covered the wound with her mouth, sucked, then turned and spat. Venom hit the floor hissing. Five times she did this, then rocked back on her heels and stroked with her hands, one up from his ankle and one down from his thigh.

Her motions swept back the luminous discoloration spreading from the wound. Each stroke forced a pulse of glowing purple-green liquid to bubble from the gash across the punctures.

Behind the venom Eanna forced from his leg, Bigger felt the blue drug expand ever more potently through his being. It advanced through his body, seeming to drive the poison to concentrate under Eanna's sweeping hands. Little by little, he felt the venom's influence give way to persistent rekeying by Entheoclone 36.

Slowly, as he watched her work, his system reanimated. Eyes alert in his unresponsive form, he tracked her actions. Feeling returned in the center of his torso, spreading first as pain that ebbed, grudgingly, from his flesh. Sensation leaked out from his core, slowly up his neck and slowly down into his fingers. Last, and most reluctantly, life moved again in his bitten leg.

He was unaware that he had begun to stir until Eanna clasped the hand he flexed unconsciously, and shushed him. Her tenderness was so astonishing that he could only gape. She patted his hand, and said, "Not too much too fast, Mr. MacGregor. I have cleared the venom, but, still, you have been bitten by a demon."

Placing his hand on his chest, she stood, and walked away. Sounds of her rummaging came from the bedroom. When she returned, she carried a painted tin the size of an old coffee can, and what looked like a cruet for chrism or salad oil. Eanna set these on the floor by the couch, and then, shifting his limbs carefully, undressed him. He shivered as his skin was exposed to air, and the shivers became violent trembling as he continued to reinvigorate.

Eanna drew down his ruined overalls in short side-to-side jerks, tugging hard until she could slide them off. When he was naked, she opened the tin, which released fragrance like heat and morning sun. He smelled clean linen, rare unguents. Dipping with her fingers, she dabbed creamy paste onto his body.

Dabbing, she told him, "It is always nice to have hope rewarded. I did not doubt that you are brave."

She dabbed his face.

"But, also, you fought well."

She rubbed the paste into his cheeks with the heels of her palms.

"A hero, Mr. MacGregor."

She patted again.

"A hero reborn."

Eanna straightened, and regarded him. He stirred, raising a hand as though he might reach for her, but she seized his wrist, gripped and released it, then moved to his feet.

Vigorously, she chafed his flesh, fast and firm, rubbing up his legs. His skin flushed red behind her touch. When she approached his groin, Bigger was disconcerted to realize he was bobbing slowly erect, but Eanna chuckled.

Leaning close to his shaft, she whispered, "Patience."

She shifted it out of the way so she could work across his hips. From there, she jumped to his near arm, and then across his chest to the other.

The effect of her effort was a surge in the sharp tingle awakening his body. With the surge came impulse to move in the parts she had warmed. His legs jerked involuntarily as Eanna worked on an arm. When she switched to the other, the one she had finished flexed on its own, bending and straightening the elbow while opening and closing a fist.

"Do that again, with your arm," she instructed.

He did.

"Again," she said. "Continue, but slowly."

The deliberate movements of his arm suppressed the involuntary twitching in his legs.

When she started on his trunk, he reached to brush a strand of hair fallen across her face, but faltered. She smiled at him, and brushed back the hair herself, then redoubled her effort. Bigger watched. Except for an occasional glance, suddenly coy, she focused intently on her task. Reaching his neck, her hands slowed, and stopped. She pulled one hand to rest over his heart, letting the fingertips of her other drift across his lips.

"Such a soft mouth," she commented to herself. "A wise mouth...."

Her voice trailed away.

He started to speak, but she laid a finger across his lips and said, "Not yet."

Raising the cruet, Eanna held it high in the diffuse light, tipping and turning it to mix faint glow into its oil. She began this time at Bigger's head. Pouring a few drops into her palm, she rubbed her hands together, raised them palm up. She anointed him, muttering as she massaged oil into his head and neck. Nine times she repeated the ritual before reaching his feet.

Life force flooded into him. Poisons blew out through the pores of his skin.

He rose onto an elbow, but Eanna objected, "Not yet."

He resisted, reaching for her. Her face softened.

"Please lie back."

Bigger stared at her until his heartbeat rose in his ears, and then he did as she asked. Eanna responded in a fluid arc of motion, pulling off her shift and straddling his thighs. She grabbed his half-awake phallus, and began to knead it with one hand. Leaning forward, she balanced the other on his chest, absorbing and reflecting his living rhythms. She peered into his eyes, intoning long, complex gutturals in a voice so harsh that, even though he watched, Bigger found it hard to credit as human. She spoke the sounds like language, and modulated her face and her tone as though making sense, but the utterances resembled nothing he had ever heard. Its cadences rang with impossible age.

Her palm warm above his heart and her hand around his enthusiastic cock erased the need for translation. She rocked forward onto her knees and sat to receive him.

Bigger waited for silence to descend and reality to shift, but it did not. Instead, he felt increasingly alert and aroused. Strength continued to flow into him. Slowly, he arched his back, pressing deeper into Eanna, lifting her.

His eyes fixed to the unbroken brown skin of her belly rising and falling as she rode him. Her belly looked so perfect that he stared, entranced. Minutes passed before it struck him that she had no navel. Not even a hint. As he formed the thought, she grabbed his chin, forcing him to look her in the face.

The surface he saw reflected back was naked lust. Desire illuminated her, making her aspect wild and startling. Behind the appetite, though, mixed other emotions, poorly cloaked and roiling among them something like worry and something like solicitude.

When he grasped this, the veil around her heart became transparent, and he realized her emotion that cut through all others was fear. She was afraid, for him. Her fear was growing. This made no sense, as he felt stronger, healthier by the instant.

They drove into the hunger, he like granite and she atop, her knees bracketing his waist, a foot tucked for leverage over each of his thighs.

Without warning, his strength drained away and he began to convulse.

Eanna shouted, "MacGregor!" and smote his face.

Silence descended as he fell. Falling and falling.

He dropped from great height, falling so far that time lost traction. It seemed he had just begun to fall, trapped in the panic of the first descent. It seemed he had been falling for hours. He fell through black, resisted only by whistling air. At one point, he feared he had begun to tumble, but he had no referent by which to judge, and no way to know if his squirming helped, or if it actually started him end-over-end. Another moment, he felt that he was not falling; rather, that he was buoyed by wind jetting from below.

Reappearance of scale was sudden and brief. Only after he shot through a cloud of ivory flecks did he realize that thousands of teeth converged on a point through which he had sped. He saw them come together in pursuit and dive, but his meteoric fall left them dwindling from sight.

Judged against that blip of detail, he realized the scale of his drop was astronomical. He need not fear the teeth because, by this point, having thought these few thoughts, he had fallen out of their world.

And then Eanna stood beside him in the black, a hand on his chest and the other covering his wound. Gradually, the rushing from below abated. Even as the wind changed from gale to whisper to nothing against Bigger's naked skin, Eanna inhabited a world becalmed. Her hands upon him, she stood firmly, feet planted, unmoving as he slowly ceased to fall.

He floated in the void. Eanna stood at his side, although on what, he could not imagine. Her hands lay motionless upon him as she matched her breath to his. When she did, they enchained, and he was powerless to breathe except with her. Inhale. Exhale. Once she ruled his lungs, her hands began to move, stroking his body in broad sweeps.

After moments—or hours—of this, he realized the sweeps were directed toward the bite on his leg. Bigger struggled up to see what she did, and discovered that he was covered by bruises. The discoloration under his skin flowed liquidly before the slight pressure of Eanna's strokes.

Only when she stopped to push him back down did it register that he floated in space, but rose from and was pushed back onto…what?

Eanna began again, now pressing a little harder. With a glance to his face, she spoke.

"The demon continues to poison you. I feared this. I fear a tooth broke off in the bite. When this happens, the fragment tunnels deep."

She paused. Pursing her lips, she stood unmoving while weighing what she said. When she went on, her hands resumed their work.

"Not into the meat, which I cleaned. Into the…," she pronounced a rasping growl.

Her brow furrowed as she cast for translation.

Finally, reluctantly, she ventured, "The…template."

She worked.

"It becomes like an abscess. Untreated, it will kill you. Or blacken your path."

Bigger lifted his head to see his leg swollen to double its normal thickness. The ghastly color Eanna swept toward the wound was sooty green. This time, as it collected, he felt a growing, throbbing burn, like the blood around the injury had begun to smolder. The throb became a pulse riding his pulse. His heartbeat pumped at the fire like a bellows. His jaw locked shut. Though he squirmed and grunted with pain, he could not cry out.

The flesh of his legs felt like liquid beginning to boil. Agony forced him rigid, a thin, protracted "squeeee" all that escaped of his scream. Eanna attempted to press on, but Belle erupted into the void. Challenge, high and tight in the dog's throat, mixed rage and uncertainty.

"I did not do this to him!" Eanna snapped. "I am trying to save him!"

Snarling and barking, Belle feinted toward Eanna, but the woman deflected her with a wave. The dog dropped low, frustration sounding deep in her chest. Eanna rested a hand on Bigger, but did nothing more. She watched Belle impatiently.

Toro emerged deliberately into their interspace from Bigger's far side, and approached. The big dog sniffed at the stricken human, and nuzzled his hand. Bigger, breathing rapidly and shallowly, almost rigid with pain, still had presence to stroke Toro's head. The dog woofed softly. When no one reacted, he walked around the couch and woofed again, more forcefully, eyes on his sister.

Slowly, Belle grew less taut. She sidled warily around Bigger's recumbent form, her eyes on Eanna as long as possible before pushing her head into her wounded human's hand. He stroked weakly. Belle whimpered. Toro trotted to his sister's side, nuzzling her in comfort.

Bigger tried to reassure them, though he could manage only, "Good...good...."

A sharp pang choked him off. Eanna gave Belle a pointed look and went back to work. Belle whimpered and sank to a crouch. Then the dogs were no longer with them, and Bigger, alone with his visitor, reclined in space.

He felt the work of her hands concentrating the pain—and presumably the poison—at the bite. Pressed into an ever smaller area, the molten burn grew more intense. When the pain concentrated to nut-size immediately under the bite, the burning drilled, auger-like, into his leg. He tried to lose consciousness to escape, but could not. Eanna kneaded his wounded flesh. Bigger screamed. The dogs matched his voice with howls from outside the bubble of void. Eanna ignored the noise and continued to force the toxin into a smaller and smaller nugget.

The pain compressed finally into an unyielding object embedded in the meat of his calf, a starburst kernel of needle-sharp spines that pierced tissue with each stroke of Eanna's hands. Bigger was aware only of misery, but Eanna's method slowly worked the object through the muscle toward the surface. The torment grew so quickly, he could not even howl.

Breathing in spastic gasps, he convulsed. His fingers strained to dig into the non-existent surface on which he writhed. Mewling from both dogs reached into the void. Then they were with him. First Belle on one side, an instant later Toro on the other, materialized from nowhere to rub against the backs of his fiercely contracted hands.

A spine broke through his skin, green-brown liquid hemorrhaging around its shaft. Eanna barked percussively, an expostulation that could only be a curse, or an oath. Frantically, she squeezed in upon the fragment with the pads of her thumbs. By sleight of hand, she produced glowing blue patches, which she slapped in a circle around the wound, adding one over his heart and one in the hollow between his brows. Reality split. Eanna twinned. The new Eanna pulled a second Bigger from inside the first.

The original Eanna continued to minister to the first Bigger, still prostrate before her. Second Bigger pulled free both vigorous and aroused. Second Eanna held the tips of his fingers as she drew him through open air to an embrace. Their mouths came together as their abdomens kissed.

Physical, voltaic, an appetite circulated between them. Lips upon Eanna's lips, Bigger slid his hand down her spine, past her buttocks to the backs of her thighs. Gently, firmly, he pulled forward, lifting her as he did. She spread her legs as he penetrated her, huffing impatiently at his restraint.

Clutching him, Eanna barked his name, "MacGregor!"

She sank down his shaft to its root. Drawing up her heels and crossing her legs, Eanna locked ankles at the small of his back. Slowly, deliberately, she pumped him, torso to torso, up and down.

Nearby, first Eanna worked desperately on first Bigger, ignoring her twin on the leaping creature that was his. First Bigger appeared comatose, all awareness shifted to his second self. First Eanna used her fingernail to split his flesh along a row of spines protruding from his leg. With the long nails of her index fingers, she pulled open the wound to expose the invasive fragment awash in green-brown liquid. Roughly spherical and covered in spines, the object throbbed with the pulse in his leg. She made no effort to extract it. Instead, she opened another dermal patch, pinched a tear in its envelope, and squeezed out the contents. The glowing blue liquid boiled as it dripped onto the bur, which began to smoke and char. A smell like scorching hair clouded around them.

The second Bigger, seeming engrossed in sex, went wide-eyed, frenzied, banging the second Eanna hard and fast. She shouted exultantly, and matched him. First Eanna, by contrast, wore a grim face as she ministered to his prostrated twin. Sweat stood on her brow. With thumb and forefinger, she held open the wound while prying the demon burr one-handed from the flesh in which it was sunk.

Careful to make sure no spine broke off, she lifted the object just enough to let her release the wound. She squeezed the last drops of blue drug from the patch. These blue dregs smoldered away the remaining spines, leaving a tiny stone, like a fossilized pea. Flicking her fingernail, first Eanna flipped this in the air and blew on it. The nugget atomized. Its dust disappeared. At last, she relaxed, and wrapped her arms around first Bigger. The moment she did, they were sucked into the heat of their seconds, and reabsorbed at full fury.

Bigger felt whole, and wholly present, for the first time since the battle. A part of him was dismayed by the flip from agony to intercourse, but Eanna allowed no time for wonder. Grabbing the back of his head with both hands, she forced open his mouth with her kiss. His eyes popped wide at her insistence. The world changed.

From a solid place in trackless void, they burst into vast space filled with stars. Bigger knew at once they were not his stars. There were too many, too densely packed, too large and radiant in a spectrum of colors impossible to describe. He gawked, certain he should not be able to perceive them.

His distraction annoyed Eanna. She gripped his cock impossibly with her cleft, breaking their kiss and binding him in a lace of arms and legs. His attention unified. He was with Eanna, probing her, arched like a bow. His heart thundered, a dance of Titans. Deaf to that earthquake, his loins drove with the shove and pull of her hips. They fucked with perfect reciprocity, together a piston, or an engine, a pumping well.

Rushing toward climax, Bigger opened his eyes to glimpse the curve of Quella's cheek fading against the background of stars, and he bucked in surprise. But then a deeper assertion, an undertone, throbbed exuberantly. He and Eanna coupled in open space, stars above, below and on every side.

He wondered how much—if any—of this was real in some verifiable way. Every singing nerve demanded that he act as though it were. Cresting to orgasm, he started to pull out, but Eanna locked her heels behind him and ground harder. They came together in a shudder. Bigger moaned pleasure through clenched teeth. Eanna shouted in triumph.

Again, Bigger expected to lose consciousness, but again it did not happen. Then he realized that he was already there, in the realm into which he had fallen before. Once more he wondered how much of this experience he hallucinated. Unaccountably, the ambiguity struck him as funny, and he grinned at the woman straddling his hips. She used both hands to tilt back his head, and poured herself into a kiss. The world went silent, and fell away, or Bigger fell. He could not determine which. There was nothing that could be known for certain except that her mouth was upon his, something or someone was falling, and his pulse sang with joy.

***

The kiss lingered on his lips like a Cheshire grin. The sense of Eanna near him faded gradually, but the feeling of her mouth on his, pressing, teasing, insistent, inviting, remained. Her kiss rode with his descent, a descent that slowed, imperceptibly at first, as it continued. He grew lighter as the fall went on. More and more featherlike, he swooped in drifting arcs, moving at behest of air currents he could not otherwise detect. Finally, he settled onto a surface, yielding but able to bear his weight.

Darkness grew less absolute, revealing that he lay on his bed. The hour was much closer to dawn than not. From the angle of its light, he knew the moon would soon disappear behind the western hills. Eanna sat beside him watching. When she saw that he was fully present, she smiled, tapped his chest once, lay down beside him and fell asleep. A cricket began to chirp somewhere in the house. Lulled by the sound, Bigger drifted off.

## IV

The sun was high and the heat well advanced when Bigger woke. Eanna was not beside him. He lay sweating onto the sheets while he took inventory of his parts.

A tapping finger proved the bite on his leg was tender to the touch, but he found no break in the skin, and no scab. He sat up to look, and could find no actual wound, only suggestive bruising. The spot pulled when he flexed the leg, and ached when it pulled, though no differently than other pangs ached and pulled on other mornings. With no more sign of injury than stiff joints, he wrote off what he remembered of the prior night to hallucination. There was probably no way to know how many blue patches Eanna had slapped onto him.

Reaching for his overalls, he froze. The left leg was torn to bloody shreds.

In the next room the dogs stirred, aware he was up. Wondering what else there was to find, he threw the ruined overalls into the laundry hamper and grabbed another pair from the chest of drawers.

Fastening a shoulder strap, Bigger crossed the living room to let the dogs out. He watched through the screen door as they descended from the porch, moving a bit stiffer than usual, he thought. The impression was brief, disappearing when the dogs had relieved themselves and begun their morning circuits of the yard.

No carcasses, demon or dog, marked the scene of the battle; however, where dead dogs might have been—if the day before had not ended in weird dream or psychotic episode—patches of ground lay bare. He was struck by how similar they looked to the lightning-blasted earth from two nights earlier. Toro sniffed the largest of the new patches before urinating on it. Facing away, he used his hind feet to scratch grass and dirt onto the spot.

If there were no dead dogs, without question there were dead chickens. Dismembered parts and bloody feathers clung to the base rail of the far fence, as though blown there by extraordinary force. Bigger could account for only eight of his hens by looking over the remains, but the wrecked coop was empty. He was disinclined to clean up the carnage. It was a task he decided would be no worse for delay. Fire ants would clear away the meat in any case.

Bigger returned to the house to start his morning routine. On his way from the bathroom to the kitchen, he spied Eanna's wooden chest on the table, and detoured without thinking. His hand stretched toward the lid as he approached, but stopped short, fingers twitching once in mid-air, at sight of a sheet of paper tucked beneath one of the box's corners.

Tri-folded like a brochure, the paper showed what appeared to be writing on its upper face, but the marks could as easily have been writerly doodles on the edge of disorder. When he took up the sheet and studied it carefully, the jots reminded him of cuneiform—if cuneiform were scrawled in ballpoint by a casual hand.

Opened, the sheet revealed a diagram in so unusual a style that Bigger had to stare before realizing it was a schematic of the flywheels in Eanna's car. Once he recognized what he held, his eyes went to the dynamic linkages that carried motion into and out of the assembly. Their basis was the same system of peristaltic transfer as in the drive shaft, which did not surprise him. What did surprise him was that he saw instantly how to do it better. Quite actually saw. Visual superimpositions on the diagram, bli-bli-blip, improvements bloomed. An additional pivot point here, supporting another rocker arm from here to here. Bigger could see the changes step up power transfer and cut inefficiency. The vision was detailed down to crosshatching to indicate depth on the new parts.

Grabbing tablet and stylus, he settled at the table to sketch, roughing in the main features of his inspiration. He managed to work out a rule-of-thumb set of specs before Toro woofed through the screen door. Time had slipped away. The dogs were hungry.

***

Scant moments after placing breakfast dishes to dry on the rack by the sink, Bigger was in the shop cutting pieces for his design. He could have printed the parts, but he liked how his imagination played as he worked lathe and laser and other tools at his bench.

Just so, only as he clamped a blank to be cut by the laser did he remember Eanna's wooden box. Finding the diagram had driven it from his thoughts. He stood away from the bench, on the verge of taking a break to inspect the box's contents, but the notion was shut down by an image of Eanna struggling to save him from the demon's bite. Her actions had earned....

Demon's bite? The tender spot on his leg pulled when he shifted his weight, but did he imagine that? Had the day before actually even happened?

Turning, he stretched, and shuffled to the bay door. The dead spots in the yard confirmed something had taken place, but no matter how long he stared, he could not see a remnant of the preternatural. Blown feathers and pieces of chicken convicted the feral pack, beyond question. Did they also indict a demon world and the bizarre man with too many teeth?

And where, now that he had stopped to ask questions, was Eanna?

A quick check showed the bike she had used before was gone. Where? Opportunity to ask had never risen. Where had she spent the previous day? Where was she now? For that matter, who was she? Somewhere in her past was a woman who had entered the hospital as a patient. How much of that person remained in the warrior-lover who had invaded his nights?

Bigger turned back to the car, stopping to study the machine as though it might give insight about its absent driver. What was he to make of her claim to have inhabited Rebecca? If the hospital staff was dosing patients with a rogue drug that induced shared hallucinations, was there risk of a contagious disorder?

The next thought stopped him. Had he been infected?

Well, he decided finally, what if? He had been given massive doses of the drug, the previous night especially. What effects could he detect?

When he took stock, he felt trashed. His body ached with a totality he had never known. Pain, unnoticed as he worked, emerged now from every joint, every muscle of his body as he explored it. In a slice of somebody's reality, he had taken a beating.

Strangely, he had not really felt the pain until he thought about it, and awareness of each shooting ache faded as soon as he ceased to pay it mind. On the other hand, his mental faculties were sharp. His imagination was in such an excited state that mere physical hurt was easy to dismiss. Two new, patentable ideas in three days. That didn't seem like fruit of a personality disorder.

The parcel delivery horn sounded from the drive. Among happy barks from Belle and Toro he heard Quella doggie-talking to them as she slid open the gate. Bigger came out of the bay wiping his hands on a shop rag as she maneuvered the pedi-van to a stop beside him.

"What a surprise!" he greeted as she stepped from the cab. "I didn't realize I had anything coming today."

"You don't, *jefe*," she informed him. "I have a package for one Eanna, last name unfortunately a blur, signature required, care of MacGregor Pedal Cars. You hiding anyone like that around here?"

Bigger ran a hand through his hair and jutted his chin at the package.

"Hiding is right. Only don't look at me. I have no idea where she spends her days."

Quella stared at him long without reacting. Bigger paled, realizing what he had said.

"But at night," she blurted, "tell me at least you're using condoms!"

The words slapped him. Before he could recover, she backed off.

"No, don't answer that! I'm sorry!"

Quella forced herself to unclench fists she had made without thinking.

"Damn it! I promised myself I'd never get jealous. We've never made a commitment."

Bigger's voice was unsteady.

"Quella, got time for a coffee? I can really use some perspective."

Again she stared at him, considering. Finally, she reached into the cab of her van and punched the monitor to show she was on break. Handing over her delivery, she collected his signature, stowed her pad, and waved toward the house.

"Lay on, MacDuff," she told him.

*** 

Over coffee, Bigger gave a narrative of events since Eanna first appeared. Much of it was vague, not because he wished to hide anything, but because he had no idea how to describe what he was not even sure had been real.

Quella let him talk until he ran down, interrupting only once to make sure she had heard the name of the drug correctly.

He finished, "…and right beside the box was a diagram that gave me the idea I was working on when you got here. Which, by the way, is going to be a game changer all by itself. With everything I've figured out in the past three days, the next roll-out will have a forty-to-sixty percent more efficient drive and better seats. I'll retrofit existing inventory. This is that big."

For a long time, she said nothing, spinning her mug.

Finally, she looked up and asked, "How sure are you that you haven't hallucinated everything, start to finish?"

In answer, he hiked his overalls and hoisted his leg onto the table. Quella inspected the bruising. Her finger barely grazed him as she traced the discoloration.

He added, "There is also a mystery car in the repair bay, not to mention a carved wooden box filled with glowing blue transdermal patches sitting there on the table by your elbow."

She jerked away.

"This box? This box!"

Quella stared.

"How did I not notice this before?"

She reached toward the lid, but pulled away before touching it.

"Okay, I'll go this far with you. Something real is happening here, but there's also a weird kind of spell, *un hechizo*, that's working."

Again, she reached as though to touch the box, but stopped, letting her hand drop to the table. She inhaled deeply, and held the breath before expelling the air. When she spoke, her words came quickly, but evenly, a considered rush.

"MacGregor, Mac, we've never talked about who we are to each other, or how that might go forward. I'm sorry to make a point of this now, but I can't let go of it. Whatever it is between us, it isn't going forward for a while."

She chewed at her lip, feeling her way forward.

"Blood donors have to wait eighteen months after questionable exposure, and then they're tested before they make another donation. I expect the same before we talk about the benefits of our friendship."

She swallowed hard, her eyes on his.

"But then I want to talk about it. If you're up for it when the time comes, I want to have that conversation."

Her shoulders rose and fell with a sigh. Bigger waited. Quella covered his hand with hers.

"In the meantime," she turned over his hand and clasped it, "Things between us have always been *muy comodo*, and I'm going to hang on to that. Now."

Her features hardened.

"As for this interlude with Little Miss Creature of the Night, I would say step one is don't let her give you any more of that drug."

Bigger started to respond, but closed his mouth. He looked long at the wooden box before nodding slowly.

When he still said nothing, Quella went on, "And it also seems to me that before you jump back in the sack...or fight any more demons...you may want to ask some pertinent questions, like her history of STIs. And, now that I think of it, what the undead use for currency when they put their cars in the shop."

"Undead?"

The word startled him.

"She's not a vampire!"

"The hell she's not!" Quella insisted. "Just looking at you, I can see she's sucking your life away. Don't go all *galante* when you're talking to me, *'chacho*. I know you too well to believe she didn't have keys to your buttons before she ever walked up the driveway."

She stood, carried her cup to the sink, and turned to contemplate the man huddled at the table. Almost, she imagined, she could follow his thoughts by the fleet expressions of his face. Bigger struggled with her words, Eanna's actions and his own confusion. Quella was sure her comments had been heard. Her tone softened.

"Mac?"

He looked up.

"*Tengo que irme.* The day doesn't get any longer."

Bigger nodded as he rose. She came around the table and put a hand on his chest.

"I won't be back this way before Tuesday unless you or...," her mouth twitched, more in a grimace than a grin, "your customer...require another delivery."

Sheepish, he embraced her. Muscular and solid, she filled his arms in a way that had felt familiar the first time they hugged. She was right. Things between them had always been *muy comodo*. He leaned forward to brush her lips, but she turned to accept the kiss on her cheek.

"Come back to me on that another time," she told him.

She started to say something else, but closed her mouth.

Then she burst out, "Look, Mac, if you need me for anything—anything! No matter what!—damn it! my phone doesn't work!—you reach me. You reach me. Promise!"

"Quella, I—"

"Promise!"

He nodded.

"Qué, I promise if you'll promise to reach me for nothing at all."

She pushed him playfully.

"No negotiation, *señor*. Stand or fall with it."

"Okay," he agreed. "I'm standing."

***

Bigger watched his friend and sometime lover pedal through the gate before returning to his shop. It was a longstanding bit of magic between them that neither watched the other out of sight when they parted. He re-entered the repair bay with more on his mind than before Quella's visit. Fortunately, the work still to be done was spelled out in design already produced. Another few pieces would complete the new assembly, after which there remained only installation in the car. With a plan for his hands, his thoughts could roam.

***

He was on the ground beneath the vehicle when Eanna returned. Her footsteps entering the bay were unmistakable. Even so, she surprised him when she leaned into the car and peered down through the uncovered transmission and flywheels in the well between the seats.

"You left this open," she announced.

"The light," was all he replied.

He gave the last bolt a final twist, slid out and stood to face her.

"You're back early."

"No."

She shook her head.

"The moon is up."

Bigger shrugged and waved toward the car as he started to turn back to it. "Let me show you what I—"

"You have had a visitor," she interrupted.

"Pardon me?"

A gesture cut off, he stood motionless, the whole of his being demanding to know what business it was of hers.

"The smell of her is thick in the yard. And inside, at the table. And on the package."

"Eanna," he began, but she held up a hand.

"I accuse you of nothing. It is the odor of talk, though beneath is affection and...hurt."

He shivered at the word, remembering Quella refusing by effort of will to be possessive.

"She brings out good in you, MacGregor."

"Eanna," he started again.

This time she waited to hear what he had to say, but he found himself at a loss for words.

"Eanna, I don't want to talk about this."

She nodded, showing no surprise.

He sniffed, and added, "There are a lot of things we ought to talk about, but this is not among them."

Eanna crossed her arms over her chest.

"What is it you wish to discuss, Mr. MacGregor?"

Bigger squelched his first response. Standing in the bay was not where he wanted to put hard questions to a testy guest. He jabbed a finger toward his day's work.

"First things first," he told her. "Right now, let's start with your car."

"Is it repaired?"

He could not or did not suppress a smile.

"More than that."

"Oh?" Eanna straightened, intrigued. "Show me."

She listened intently as he explained what had failed and why. Leaning into the cab beside him, she followed his description while peering at the works in the transmission well. When he began to discuss the relative efficiencies of the modifications he had made and those still planned, she stood out from the car, causing him to follow in order to continue talking. She interrupted once.

"In my car you have put these things?"

"Yes," he confirmed. "First versions of prototypes. If you don't like the results, I can still switch it all back. I haven't cannibalized or recycled anything."

She answered by pushing him aside with the back of a hand. In one motion, she snapped the cowl over the transmission well as she slid into the driver's seat. Bigger's eyes went to her leg as she drew it into the cab.

"You changed the seat," she noted, testing the fit.

"Better," she pronounced. "I like this."

As she eased backward from the slip at his tool bench, he held his breath, waiting for reaction. When she nodded, though to herself, he exhaled.

Churning dust from the floor, she accelerated backward out of the bay with no warning. Eanna slewed the car ninety degrees as she flashed into the sun, skidded to a stop, and shifted gears. The car leapt forward. Bigger ran from the bay to see her cross the yard and exit the gate. He had a moment of panic that she was fleeing, but then remembered she had neither the wooden chest nor her suitcase. He followed through the gate and ambled down the drive to watch as she put the car through its paces.

He was unsurprised that she was a demanding driver. For purely selfish reasons, it suited him that her idea of checking his handiwork pushed the car to the edge of its tolerances. Speeding past for the third time, she gave him a "thumbs up." The next pass, she blew a kiss through the vee of her fingers. The next time, she skidded to a stop before him, popped open her window and said, "Get in. I want to know how it handles with two of us."

Bigger folded into the passenger seat as Eanna flipped a lever to engage the pedals on his side. He was still situating himself when she let out the clutch and jumped them forward, flashing him a vulpine grin. Instantly, she was pedaling hard, pumping energy into the flywheels to power their acceleration. Wearing a grin to rival hers, Bigger leaned into pedals, matching Eanna pump for pump. In minutes, they left the dirt road that crossed Bigger's land and shot onto the county asphalt. Landscape tore past.

Cresting a steep rise, they found the man with too many teeth blocked their way. Eanna did not break or swerve, instead plowing straight ahead. The man dove for the shoulder. Bigger laughed, stroked a point in the air, then looked back. There was no sign of the man. Tall grass beside the road waved in the wind, revealing nothing of what it may or may not have hidden.

Settling back in his seat, he saw Eanna watched him sidelong, bemusement on her face.

"What?" he demanded.

She smiled as though something had been confirmed, but ignored his question when she spoke.

"The sound is different. And never have I managed such speed. Clearly, the repair is successful. The modifications are good. I commend you."

Her praise was welcome, but he chose not to acknowledge it, changing the subject instead.

"After the past couple of days, I would think that you could call me Bigger."

"No," she refused. "That is not a dignified name."

He started to reply, but the road opened at an intersection. Eanna threw the car out of gear, gripped the handbrakes, and wrested the juddering car through a doughnut to return the way they had come. Bigger threw up a hand to brace against the frame of the cowling, but she still knocked into him.

"Well," he observed. "That bit of technique didn't snap the drivetrain. We'll call that a plus. I'm glad you're giving her a workout."

"What do you mean?"

She glared at him with sudden suspicion.

"Who do you mean? Her? You said 'her.' Is this working out that woman?"

Bigger stared at her. She turned back to the road.

"Do not gape," she said peevishly. "Her trace is like a fog around your table."

He faced forward, watching the packed cinder roadway roll beneath them. Neither said anything else until they re-entered the yard, when Bigger spoke.

"Pull into the bay, if you will. I'd like to check that everything is trim and tight."

Eanna smirked as she slowed to maneuver.

"The car, you mean."

He blushed, but answered without his voice breaking.

"The car, of course. Yes."

A moment later, he added, "Absolutely."

Bigger himself pulled the vehicle onto the raised tracks of the slip beside his workbench. Curious that his heart pounded only now, he sat watching in the rearview mirror until Eanna disappeared out the door of the bay.

It was a quick matter to check the bolts and pins he had placed, but he lingered over the entire car. Once done, he reversed it off the tracks, pulled out and turned around, backing it under cover for the night.

The dogs sprawled on either side of the doormat when he climbed the steps onto the porch. He was momentarily pleased that they were not inside with Eanna, but this turned to concern when he realized both were so deeply asleep that his approach did not rouse them. Concern became fear when he patted first Belle, then Toro, and neither responded to his touch.

Yanking open the door, he leapt across the threshold, and stopped cold. The man with too many teeth was at the dining table, Eanna directly across from him. Bigger's entrance went completely unremarked.

The pair sat, eyes locked, silent, but with tension between them that swarmed the room like hornets. Eanna's box of drugs sat on the table directly in front of the man, who looked unmistakably smug. Eanna's glare was poison. She sat motionless with rage.

Bigger felt lethargy overtake him. It grew, coming like a tide, from which the scene at the table seemed to retreat. Normal sounds of the house grew muffled and distant.

"No!" he mutely refused.

Shuddering physically, he threw off the torpor and strained toward ordinary space. Ponderously, as though through wet cement, he dragged his senses closer to normal perception.

For the first time the intruder acknowledged Bigger, astonished eyes snapping to the latecomer. In a blink, Eanna threw herself onto the table, snatched the box, and rolled back to her chair, her prize clutched to her chest.

Shrieking, the man turned on her. Throwing his arms wide, he gaped his mouth. From the maw erupted a vortex of teeth that obscured the ceiling.

Eanna swung an arm to ward off teeth. Some grew to enormous size. Thousands split into finer and finer gnashing slivers. She struggled to open the chest with her other hand, but the clasp would not yield. Her movements became desperate when the teeth struck.

Bigger recoiled when teeth flew from the intruder's mouth, but his outrage went instantly critical. This monster was in his house. Ignoring the storm of teeth, he charged, leaping to hit the adversary with a flying tackle that carried both of them into one of the dining chairs, shattering it.

The teeth evaporated when Bigger struck, but the man himself remained unmistakably solid. Bigger landed heavily, his breath knocked away. He saw the man rise, pick up a chair leg and start toward him, but through the man's legs he saw Eanna, no longer menaced by the teeth, throw open the box, snatch out a patch, peel it and slap it on. Her giant warrior self burst forth.

The intruder rose onto his toes, raising the chair leg to club Bigger, but before he could strike, Eanna was on him. It was all Bigger could do to roll away from their stomping feet.

He strained to recover, forcing his diaphragm to still against his body's desperate need for air, and then forcing himself to inhale slowly and deeply. He rose carefully, pausing half-bent, hands on knees, before pulling himself erect to rejoin the battle.

The man had grown as large as warrior Eanna, and fought with mad glee on his face. Warrior Eanna's features were cold determination, but Bigger saw her human-sized self against the wall, forearms sporting twin rows of dermal patches. She hunched low with desperation. The battle went badly.

He was at a loss for a way to help her, but the smaller Eanna waved him close. He went to her, skirting the giant fighters by hugging the wall. She rummaged in the chest as he came up beside her, and when he was in reach, slapped a patch onto his arm. He felt the drug enter his system. The world began to shift, but he tore away the patch and discarded it.

"No!" he barked. "No more of that!"

She gave him an imploring look, but he shook his head emphatically. Her shoulders sagged. Bruises marked half her face and one eye was swollen almost shut. Beneath the patches on her arms were more bruises that looked like she had wrested free from an iron grip. Blows her enemy aimed at the giant warrior were striking the mortal woman. Obviously, the projection, or whatever it was, was failing.

As he watched, her head snapped hard against the wall, followed instantly by the intruder's roar of triumph. Bigger spun to see warrior Eanna broken backward across the table, her form beginning to disintegrate, her particles vanish.

The intruder hung over his evaporating foe, triumph preternaturally splitting his face. Grinning, he watched until nothing remained of the warrior but an atomizing shell, and then, slowly, his gaze rose to Bigger shivering at the edge of panic.

Huge, strapping, the man with too many teeth moved without hurry to circle the table. Casting about for a weapon, Bigger snatched the chest from stunned Eanna's hands and brandished it. His enemy charged.

Bigger spun, rising onto his toes, and smashed the box against the giant's head. The ancient wood splintered, blue-glowing patches and fragments of wood raining across the room. The intruder buckled, falling backward to the floor, knocked out cold.

As Bigger watched, his monstrous adversary shrank to ordinary size, the unnatural maw reforming to a shape more or less normal. Or slightly wider than normal. The mortal taking shape still had a big mouth. Eyebrows sprouted over his eyes. A fine stubble appeared on his scalp and jaw. A jagged gash where Bigger had struck him began to bleed copiously.

Fascinated by the transformation happening on his floor, Bigger suddenly recognized the man as an orderly from the hospital. He flushed with new anger. At the same time, he worried the bastard was bleeding to death, and lost minutes undecided whether to stanch his wound or tie him up.

Eanna's moan drove the man from his thoughts.

Kneeling at her side, he took her wrist in hand and checked her pulse. For an instant, it seemed weak and erratic, but it steadied, strengthening so quickly that he doubted his first impression.

"Eanna," he said softly.

Her eyelids fluttered.

He spoke her name again, and this time she opened her eyes, although it took a moment for them to focus. When they did, she smiled weakly.

Gingerly, she turned her head to look around, taking in the bloody figure sprawled beyond Bigger, the burst wood of the chest, and the scattered dermal patches. Her eyes opened wide at the sight. Bigger turned to survey the mess. A name floated up from memory.

"Kenny," he pronounced.

"Do not name him!" Eanna pleaded, but the emotion taxed her. Less forcefully, she asked, "You know the man he uses?"

"Yes and no," Bigger answered. "I remember the name on his scrubs."

Flushing angrily, he added, "I'll name him all right. As soon as a posse can get here."

"You understand nothing," his guest insisted.

Closing her eyes, she inhaled deeply, catching at a pang in her chest. She lifted a hand.

"Help me up."

Maneuvering an arm around her, he raised the injured woman from the floor. It was apparent that her legs would not yet hold her weight, and she gasped when he embraced her bruised ribs to lift her.

Uncertain, he stopped.

"Eanna?" he asked, but she shook her head and managed through gritted teeth, "The couch."

She staggered as he guided her around the bloodied figure on the floor. His gentleness when lowering her to the couch earned a smile, which he took as a sign of recovery. Bigger hovered while Eanna situated herself. At a sound from behind, he spun.

The man was sitting up, a hand pressed to his head wound. Bigger he spared a sneering glance, and glared longer at Eanna. The splintered wood, broken vials and dermal patches on the floor around him got a long, searching look.

"Don't move!" Bigger commanded.

Other than an expression of contempt, the man hardly bothered to react. His eyes fixed on the largest remnant of the box, sitting amidst glass shards and blue patches.

Eanna snarled in the guttural tongue.

In English, she spat, "I did not steal them! You lost them, pig!"

"To your bottle!"

The man's voice was sandpaper on brass.

"And you drained it!" she rejoined. "Drunkard!"

A wave of sadness washed over his face. His head bobbed, admitting her truth.

The moment evaporated. He lunged onto his feet. Snatching a patch, he tore away its backing and slapped it to his neck.

Surprised, Bigger was still crouching to react when the man bucked and snorted at the jolt of the drug. Bigger started forward, but the man bowled him aside, charging past. The screen door burst as he went through it.

By the time Bigger made it to the porch, the man was nowhere in sight. An empty yard confronted him, inscrutable in its ordinariness. From the top of the steps, Bigger listened, hoping to hear what he could not see. What he heard was Toro's groan behind him.

The big dog lay as before, but his eyes were open. Only when Bigger knelt did he notice the fletching of a tiny dart in the dog's flank. He snatched it out and cast it against the wall, the point wedging into the siding with a "snick!" He pulled a dart from Belle's side and flung it to stick in the porch rail. She blinked, and one of her forelegs twitched as she woke.

Bigger stroked her neck, his hand coming to rest on her shoulder. Settling onto his knees, he placed his other hand on Toro. From the shattered door, Eanna watched Bigger trying to will strength into his dogs.

"MacGregor," the woman called softly.

He did not answer right away, concentrating on deep, measured breaths.

At last, he said, "Yeah?"

"MacGregor," she repeated, but paused, then pronounced, almost in a whisper, "Bigger."

Lifting his head, he did not look directly at her, but listened. She continued in a surprising voice, almost hesitant, almost tender.

"Since they are not dead, they will recover."

He made no move away from the dogs, gazing at nothing. In full, slow rhythm, he breathed in and out.

"You must believe me," Eanna pressed. "My time with you grows short. The moon is high and the sun goes down."

The light told him evening approached, but he looked over his shoulder for confirmation anyway.

More urgently, Eanna began, "Bigger MacGregor, your friends are no ordinary animals—"

"Don't you think I know that?" he cut her off.

She let the challenge pass, speaking husky and low.

"Bigger, please. I need you."

He stood.

"Of course," he answered, but his eyes remained on his dogs.

Only when a tiny mew escaped her did he glance up.

"Eanna!" he cried, and jumped to catch her as she sagged down the doorframe.

Pulling her arm around his neck and drawing her close, Bigger shouldered her weight and started toward the couch. She redirected.

"The bed. Please."

Steering her was awkward. Her limbs—and all the rest of her—responded unpredictably when she tried to walk. She would manage a controlled step, lurch to the side, then catch herself, sagging against him. Finally, Bigger swept her up and carried her into the bedroom, letting her concentrate on clinging to his neck.

Eanna held on until he lowered her atop the comforter, kneeling against the bed to place her without jarring. She curled onto her side.

As he stood away, she said without turning to look, "Don't go. Please. Lie down and hold me."

Fleeting thoughts of a glass of water, aspirin, some other aid, came and went. Instead, he kicked off his shoes and slid onto the bed. Eanna drew up her legs, inviting him to spoon. Bigger slipped an arm beneath her neck and draped the other along her side. Pulling it around, she cupped his hand lightly to her breast. The touch calmed her, and she dozed.

Her face turned, the sound of her breathing drifted across a pillow before coming back to him like the rote of faraway surf. Its muted regularity lulled him to drift with the faint double-bump of her heart. As the afternoon glare softened to gold, they hardly moved. Bigger closed his eyes for only a second, or so it seemed, and the light turned lazuli. A moment later, he blinked, and lay in the silvered gloom of night.

A particle of his brain remained awake to hear toenails click on decking, then floor, as Toro and Belle moved inside the open front door. Toro groaned as he was wont to do when settling. Belle, as always, was flat against the floor when she sighed. Bigger registered these things even as the warmth of the woman he held conspired with the lulling of crickets in the yard.

One moment, he thought, "Frogs," and smiled.

There had been rain, and there were frogs. One did not hear them much anymore. Bigger did not think about that. He thought, "Frogs," and was pleased. Adjusting his arms around Eanna, he muttered something sentence-like, but meaningless, falling silent as his breathing drifted again into synchrony with hers. Her answer was a tiny panting sound, but she did not wake. The wakeful particle of his brain relaxed.

He had drowsed deeply when Eanna pushed back with her bottom against the unconscious twitch of an emerging hard-on. Her hand crept back, sliding between the curves of her butt and the denim of his overalls. His eyes snapped open. She molded her palm and fingers to his stiffening response.

"You come around quickly," he whispered.

"You understand nothing," she stated matter of factly, stroking the bulge at his crotch.

Bigger slid his hand from her breast to her belly, pressing gently to pull her tighter against him. Luck made his fingers deft as he slipped the button and slowly lowered the zipper of her pants. She inhaled sharply when his fingers stroked down her body into the swell between her thighs. Little by little, he eased his middle finger inside her.

Eanna withdrew her hand and leaned her upper body away, forcing her butt against his crotch. Huffing rapidly, impatiently, she fidgeted to push her pants to her knees. At first, she clutched his side to stop him when he moved to get up, but relented when she saw no graceful, sensual way to get him out of his overalls. He took the opportunity to visit the bathroom, returning with the straps off his shoulders, his t-shirt gone, the overalls falling low as he unrolled a condom onto his penis. Eanna spied the rubber and laughed.

"Now you have regrets?" she asked.

He did not meet her eye. With a wiggle, he shed overalls and stepped from the garment as it piled around his feet. Eanna kept her back resolutely to him, lying in an S-curve that cried out for embrace.

As he slid onto the bed, she shifted, backing her rump tight against him. His arm beneath her cradled her head; the other he folded around to stroke her belly, but she seized his hand and pulled it to her chest.

Circling her bottom in a slow, teasing press, she reached through her legs to draw his erection between her thighs, gripping him hard against her crotch. Bigger's breathing quickened, but Eanna's motions remained unhurried. The way she held him allowed no leverage to push for a faster pace.

Each time Eanna shoved back, her fingertip traced along his shaft to the scar of its lost foreskin. His erection hardened. Bigger grabbed her hip and strained to push through the clench of her thighs. He could not press forward. He had no wish to draw back.

Fingers and thumb, she played a downy touch over the latex sheath on his bucking phallus. Lightly, she pinched the tip, then pushed her hand between his erection and her crotch to penetrate herself with a finger. She withdrew it, moist, aromatic, and began to paint the straining rubber with her juices. Bigger moaned, released her hip, and pulled his belly away from the cheeks of her ass. Eanna rolled slightly forward, and cupped the head of his cock against the lips of her vagina. She rocked back. Like that, he was inside her.

He expected the world to fall away, or stand still, or open into undreamed displays of color. It did not. Heartbeat and breath thrummed in his ears, but as heart and breath. A familiar ecstasy. Eanna remained singular, tangible. The bed remained a bed.

Rigid, transfixed, he panted.

Eanna's chest heaved. Her nostrils flared as he enlarged inside her. She felt his push, harder, deeper, when she squeezed, and she felt the tension shift in his thighs when he began to draw back. With a cry, she ground hard, forcing him flat as she rolled on top. Astraddle his hips, facing his feet, she was off, rhythmically at first, then bouncing wildly. Released by this new position, Bigger pressed steadily upward, rocking beneath the slap of her flesh. Eanna ruthlessly pounded him. She growled hoarse, ferocious joy.

Arching from the bed as much as her intensity allowed, Bigger tightened his buttocks as he tried to force himself higher, deeper, farther inside. He raised hands to her hips, but she knocked them away, and knocked them away again when his palms drifted to her thighs. Eanna grinned, and pushed his arms down, pinning him as she sped fucking to a gallop.

Bracing harder, Bigger watched without flinching, biding until pleasure caused her guard to drop. With the sweep of an arm and buck of a leg, he rolled her onto her back and pushed into her. For an instant, locked crotch to crotch, he spasmed, straining deeper, but then he drew back and plunged forward, and then again, and then faster, and faster. Eanna shouted new challenge as she drew up her legs and spread to absorb his reciprocating jabs. He fucked her with deep, unhesitating strokes, his breathing metrical, a distance runner hitting stride. Eanna gasped and shouted as she threw herself roughly against him, a flood checked but not pacified.

Then they found it, the angle, the delirious pace, the synchronization that opened a path to climax. Once on it, they effortlessly matched, two halves of an engine driving to purpose. Her arms went around his neck. She melded against his body. Their mouths bruised when lips sought imperative lips.

Bigger shoved her into the bed with every push. She wound arms and legs around him, formed to his body, gripping him tight within and without. Her voice to his ear, she spurred him. Harsh, explosive syllables formed words, or apparent words, in a language he did not know. Her heels drove against his ass. Together they shrank to the single dimension of skin on skin. A roar swept over them. The sounds of the world washed away.

They came together, locked rigid by spasms jolting through two bodies incapable of separate response.

Bigger felt the condom burst when he ejaculated, but was powerless to react. In the aftermath, he sagged, momentarily pinning Eanna with his weight. She shifted her interrogatively, but he rolled off and gazed down at flesh peeking through torn latex.

She raised his face and gave him a peck on the nose, saying simply, "You understand nothing."

There was an implicit question when she touched a finger to the moist head of his cock, but he was spent and she did not press. She held him with tender arms as he sank near dozing.

Instead of tipping into sleep, however, he roused. Rising onto an elbow, he tossed off the heaviness with a shake of his head, and pushed her onto her back so that he could look at her.

"MacGregor," she mouthed.

He arched an eyebrow at his name. Instead of letting him answer, she pulled herself into a sitting position and placed a finger across his lips. Her head tucked over his, she drew him close. Cradled by her arms, his ear at the base of her neck, he listened to the whoosh of her pulse, and the steady murmur of her heart beneath.

Beat by beat, he traveled with her into peace, then stillness, then sleep.

***

It seemed only an instant had passed when he opened his eyes, but utter darkness told him the sky was lit by the last stars of night. He was alone.

Climbing back into his overalls, he strode from the bedroom and stopped. The drugs and wreck of the box were gone. Pieces of smashed chair remained where they had fallen. His dogs sat alert by the table, watching him.

Belle woofed when Bigger started for the door. He waved her off and went out to the porch. She followed, moving ahead as they crossed the yard to the shop. Toro stayed where he sat.

Her car was gone. The emptiness in the bay where it had been was already ambiguous. He could have missed her by an hour or by five minutes.

Turning on lights in the shop revealed how few traces of her remained, and those were actually his own traces. A crude sketch hung next to where he propped his notebook. Curls of silver metal glinted beside the lathe.

He turned on all the lights, including the exterior floods, and stood gazing into the yard, from which she was equally absent. The light provoked motion under the porch. He squinted to make out the cause.

Tilting her head first right, then left, the little red hen peeked tentatively from beneath the steps. With a shout, Bigger rushed to sweep her up, Belle loping beside him, but as he approached, the hen retreated. She settled onto a clutch of eggs Bigger dropped to hands and knees to see. Belle crept into the low space and plopped alongside the expectant mother, nuzzling her gently. The hen did not protest, but began a quiet clucking commentary to which the dog seemed to give full attention. A lump in his throat, Bigger stood, dusted his knees and started into the house.

Toro still waited beside the table, if not patiently, then at least without fuss. He sat alert on his haunches, as though marking time while Bigger went through the motions of proving what he already knew. Eanna had gone. Briefly, dog and man locked eyes, then the dog licked his lips and stretched. Groaning his familiar groan, Toro lay down heavily, exuding a sense that—obviously—the fact that he waited where he did could only mean it was a place with answers.

Bigger studied the animal for clues to the reality of previous days. Toro was as self-contained as ever, sprawled with head flat on the floor for the cooler air. Without lifting his muzzle, the dog looked pointedly from Bigger to the table. Bigger looked, too. At the place the box had occupied across three days was a pouch. Beneath the pouch, double-folded, was a sheet of his own stationery.

Stepping over his dog, Bigger prodded the round belly of the pouch. Full and heavy, it sounded like it held ball bearings or buckshot. Before investigating the contents, however, he took up the paper. Two blue-glowing, transdermal patches were tucked into the first fold. The opened sheet held a couple rows of wedge-shaped scrawls, dashed off in haphazard cuneiform. He could picture her beside the table, jotting the note without ever thinking that the scratches would mean nothing to him.

The pouch was leather. Scarring on the hide revealed that, like the seats in her car, it was skin from an actual life and not out of a vat. The source of the clicking proved to be what looked at first like beads. He lifted one out and swatted a light switch.

An egg-shaped pellet of gold rested in his hand. Four of them would cover his thumbnail. There was no perforation, so it had not been cast as a bead. Pouring a handful into his palm, he saw all were gold, all were the same in every detail, identical even in close inspection. It was gold of exceptional purity. Some of these would go to uses other than commerce.

Guessing at the volume of pouch and contents, Bigger decided she had left him nearly a liter of gold pellets. Around the waist of each was embossed a ring of tiny, eight-pointed stars, which sent him back to the note. Scrawled at the bottom was the same eight-pointed star. It was almost eclipsed by a final symbol, which he did not recognize at first was a smiley-face.

Bigger was stuck, puzzling between gold pellets in one hand and an unreadable note in the other. It was clear the episode with Eanna, whoever she may have been, was over. Cashed out and accounts settled. What came next, what action he needed to take right that minute, was not apparent. Stuck between floods of regret and relief, he could not see the steps from where he stood to breakfast.

Even so, vibrating deep inside, he felt a current of excitement. Beauty, passion, war had come and gone. His discoveries remained. Technical consequences of her visit would shape his work for years to come.

Lost in thought, he was staring vacantly at the tiny forms in his hand when the lights of an approaching vehicle swept across the windows. Bigger returned the beads to the pouch, and dropped the pouch in a drawer of his sideboard before heading to the yard. When he saw the headlights at the gate, he knew it was Quella. Toro brushed by to greet her. Belle rose to join her brother, passing Bigger on the steps.

"Early start?" Bigger called.

"No start yet," Quella answered, stepping from her van. "Somehow my phone started working again, just in time to receive a text from an unidentified source."

She stood waiting as he neared.

"Unidentified source?" he fished. "I didn't know that was even possible any more."

"Don't kid, Mac."

She studied him. Worry showed on her face.

"Five words. 'I return him to you.'"

He rocked back.

"That's it?"

"That's it."

She flushed, but did not look away.

"I needed to know you hadn't bled to death after that bitch tore out your throat with her canines."

He smiled wistfully, his gaze drifting to look over Quella's shoulder at nothing. She reached for his chin and turned his face until she looked in his eyes.

Peering there, she said at last, "I think your throat was the least of my worries."

"Actually."

He pulled her hand from his face and held it.

"Actually," he said again, "There was a risk."

He looked toward the ruined coop.

"More than a little. I'm glad you worried."

"Her bill?" Quella asked.

"Paid. Generously."

"Generously?"

"Gold was only the start."

"Ah, you learned. You have new ideas?"

Bigger turned, drawing Quella by the hand.

"Let me make some coffee," he said. "If you don't mind an earful, I'd like to ramble about how I plan to change the world."

He stopped, swiped the air, and reframed.

"How I plan to change the world…of pedal cars."

"The world," Quella repeated softly.

Slipping an arm around his waist, she tugged.

"The day doesn't wait, Mac, and neither does my route. I'll give you an hour."

The End

# Death on the Toilet

Bigger MacGregor stood at the window of the home he shared with his youngest granddaughter and her son, remembering a strip of mixed growth that had taken a decade to bring back from naked caliche. A narrow band of restored savanna, it had been the pride of the entire MacGregor family. His granddaughter, Anna, was just old enough to remember the wildflowers. But then the adjoining woods had been claimed under extra-territorial jurisdiction, and the MacGregor edge was seized as right-of-way. Destruction of both woods and strip had been the willful act of an outfit called Tremaine Developments.

Eighty-two years old and a restless sleeper, Bigger stopped at the window at least once a night to grieve for his lost savanna. Each time, he recalled pieties about "expanding tax base" and "making fallow lands profitable" thrown back in the face of every protest by fat, cigar-chomping Duane Tremaine III.

Turning from the window, Bigger opened his bathroom door to find Death on the toilet. The old man stared, expecting the spectral form to resolve into his great grandson, Paulie, or, failing that, into some other mundane presence, perhaps a burglar. The figure, however, remained what it was, hood angled toward Bigger in a way that seemed to return his gaze.

"So, is this it, then?" Bigger asked.

The figure shook its head, extending an arm. Folds of its robe spread as it did so, becoming the feathers of an enormous wing. A hundred eyes peered from midnight plumage, winking slowly, asynchronously. They studied the man, who blinked and studied back.

Suddenly, most of the eyes clenched shut, and the figure hunched upon itself. Bigger heard, or imagined he heard, a ghost of the sound of bowels voiding. A smell like concentrated calla lilies forced him back, into the hall. The many eyes opened again, appearing drained. Impressions not of his making formed in MacGregor's mind as he struggled to interpret a message from beyond life's pale.

*"Unexpected stop. A consequence of working closely with Pestilence."*

From the black within its hood came a sound like Death moistening its lips. Bigger wondered about the etiquette of the situation, whether or not he should offer a glass of water, but he had no opportunity. The figure strained again, its arm contracting as the effort forced shut its eyes. The smell of callas billowed out as Death again voided.

*"Umnh!"* took shape in Bigger's mind. His own guts gurgled in sympathy.

A moment later, the figure regained its poise, if poise may be ascribed to Fatality. It refastened its eyes on its accidental host. After a hesitant instant, words articulated soundlessly in the mortal's head.

*"There is an appointment that must be kept."*

The specter pointed to a scythe leaning against the wall. Bigger was sure no scythe had been there an instant before. He nodded toward it.

"No man waits for Death?" he asked.

The figure shook its hooded head.

*"Hardly original."*

Even silent, the observation was weary.

*"No matter. Your assistance is needed."*

"Mine?"

MacGregor's thoughts raced.

"You want me to sub for you?"

The Reaper nodded, pointing more emphatically to its implement.

"I'm hardly qualified," the man objected. "I'd have no idea what to do."

Death jabbed its finger forcefully, its silent voice ringing inside the mortal's skull.

*"The scythe will lead."*

Bigger looked from the honed edge of blue-black metal to the figure on the commode.

"Are you asking me as a favor?"

Death shook its head, and jabbed once more, but was overtaken by a spasm of voiding. Bigger snorted.

"You think just because you have the runs you can draft any convenient body to handle your gig?"

Nodding, the specter nodded pointed once more to the scythe.

"I don't think so," declined Bigger. "I have no idea how to harvest somebody's life."

He started to retreat from the bathroom, but the world stretched in a disorienting way. He found himself outdoors, clad in Death's garment, clasping the tool of Death's trade.

Inside his head, an echo faded, *"The blade will lead. Follow the blade...."*

As if this were a cue, the scythe pulled MacGregor toward the scar of ground that had once been the back third of his yard. The crews of Tremaine Developments had dug out the strip to a depth of nine feet, making drainage for a gated subdivision that now occupied fifty acres of one-time forest. The Reaper's blade drew the man toward the lip of this ditch, to an enormous cottonwood that had struggled to hold on, sacrificing more boughs month by month as it clung to existence. Only the day before, Bigger had noted that a single branch remained in leaf, and that last foliage had not looked healthy.

As he stepped beside the tree, the scythe came around of its own accord, sweeping in an unhurried, stately arc through the trunk. It met no resistance. When the blade had passed through, the trunk seemed unmarked, but a second later the remaining leaves let go with tiny pops, faint, but clearly audible to death-heightened ears.

Astonished, Bigger felt life depart the tree. It came through him like a focused beam, a tight flow of energy moving as sedately as the stroke that released it. Its passage imparted a charge that both diffused through his body and concentrated in the blade.

"Not so bad," he thought with relief, turning back toward the house.

The scythe followed other intentions.

Bigger was yanked away from the tree and toward a small luminescence converging on another, even smaller. Though pulled at inconceivable speed, he knew the traces as a screech owl snatching a vole. Violence that would have dislocated his shoulders had he not stood proxy for Death swept the blade in churning strokes that paced the talons of the owl.

The rodent died shrieking. Its life, wee though it was, rocketed up Bigger's arms and burst from his back.

"An appointment!" he yelled to the night. "You said 'an appointment.' That was two!"

The contrast between the deaths of the vole and the tree could not have been greater. This tiny demise, going through him like a pellet, was an outrage. He felt corrupted by the brutal turbulence of the event. Whatever the creature's vitality may have been, it had gone through Bigger with pain and fear, rather than release as that of the tree had done. And yet, like that of the tree, the vole's death had given him energy. Even more, it had energized the scythe.

Confused, Bigger tried again to turn home. When the Reaper's instrument still pulled him in another direction, he flung it, opening his grasp to let it fall where it might. The fatal tool, however, would not leave his hands. Despite the strength with which he shoved, the smooth grain of its stock remained solidly against his palms. What was more, it drew him inexorably toward a third appointment.

Ironically—at least it seemed to him ironic— the line he traveled was the ditch where his beloved strip of wild had been. He moved through the air nine feet above ditch-bottom, as though his role as Death's stand-in forced him to travel the ghost of a disappeared landscape.

In passing, he felt, with a clarity absolute and unmistakable, the signature of each organism that had been snuffed during the excavation. Every extinguished clump of grass, every uprooted shrub, every broken insect whispered its identity. In their thousands, he grieved for them.

Though his speed was blinding, he was hounded by ectoplasmic traces of lost savanna. Minuscule haunts beyond number made a journey of forty yards seem to take forever.

At last, he passed into the new subdivision. Thankfully, he was spared haunting from the myriad victims of that constructed habitat. Drawn by the scythe, he flashed toward a third encounter.

An instant later he stood before a house, the largest and most obviously customized amid blocks of repeating floor plans. Without ever having been there, Bigger knew this was the home of Duane Tremaine III, the developer who had destroyed his woodland edge. Rage and grief surged together in his core, but he hardly registered the storm of emotion before he found himself inside the house. For a heartbeat, he paused in the entry, just within the door. Another heartbeat placed him at the foot of Tremaine's bed. The corpulent developer lay upon it, less asleep than unconscious, laboring to breathe.

As MacGregor realized he was again watching the final instants of a life, the scythe spasmed in his hands. The shock of it thrashed his arms. Clearly the implement had brought him to an appointment with fury. The razor steel hungered toward the energy it was about to release.

"No!" MacGregor shouted, throwing himself back as the blade bucked forward.

When it jerked right, Bigger, tensing will more than muscles, twisted left. Answering, the scythe arced over his head. Body frail with eighty-two years but his determination hardened by a lifetime, he knew that conviction rather than sinew was his strength.

The scythe swooped to kill. The old man threw himself backward and rolled. He came up on his feet facing away from the deathbed, the implement braced before him, its curving edge looming above his head. In an instant, he knew that his age meant nothing in this struggle. If Death's blade was preternatural steel, the spirit of Bigger MacGregor was adamantine. He would not be forced to carve even his enemy.

The scythe did not yield. It was incapable of yielding, but in this moment so was the one charged to carry it. Bigger turned carefully, inflexible grip on the instrument straining to slice. With hard-won deliberateness, he let the point sink unhurried toward its target's chest. He could not impart grace to the movement, nor dignity, but, really, he had no interest in granting the developer a graceful or dignified death. What he could do, and what he did, was allow Duane Tremaine III to go quietly into never-ending night.

The blade sank into the expiring body, its fury pent as its tip entered a floundering heart. Bigger held it motionless for a fraction of a second, refusing to allow the steel to rend and shred. Then, as life flowed up and out, he passed the razor curve through the new corpse in a single, smooth stroke. The developer's livingness washed through both old man and implement, and flowed on to wherever it went. Already dead, Tremaine's body gave up its last breath with a nearly inaudible sigh.

MacGregor wasted no time over the body. He turned and stepped toward the door to the room. Immediately, he was outside. Another step found him at the lip of the ditch, and another found him back in the hall of his home, at the door of the bathroom. Death waited there, eyes hidden in plumage again folded close like the deep sleeves of a robe.

Bigger held out the scythe, and Death took it. For a moment the specter regarded him with apparent curiosity.

When the figure turned to leave, the man said, "Guess I'll see you soon."

Death paused, seeming to hesitate. Once more, words formed in Bigger's mind.

*"Not today."*

The mortal nodded. The Reaper turned away, fading as it did so. No trace remained of its time in the bathroom except an overwhelming smell of calla lilies.

***

MacGregor stood fixed in thought until a small voice interrupted.

"Papa?"

His great grandson peered from the end of the hall.

"Paulie?" Bigger asked. "What are you doing up?"

"Papa, I had a dream. It scared me."

The old man knelt, opening his arms.

"I'm sorry, little one. Come on. Let's go in the den, and I'll rock you to sleep."

Stepping into Bigger's embrace, the boy sniffed.

"Papa," he asked, "What's that smell?"

"Flowers, I think."

Bigger sniffed, too.

"Nothing to worry about. It'll be gone by morning."

***

Daybreak found man and boy asleep in the rocker, the child's head against MacGregor's chest. Anna woke her grandfather when she lifted her son.

"Papa, are you all right?" she asked.

"I think so, sweetie."

Bigger stretched, making his joints crack.

"We just had dreams."

***

It was another day in another season before Death came for Bigger MacGregor. The passing was not entirely painless, and it did not happen when he was asleep, but as much as Death allowed, the old man managed it with dignity and grace. Anna lifted a dozing Paulie from his lap scarcely ten minutes before Bigger, again in the rocker, breathed his last.

Years later, Paulie would recall that his great grandfather had been wrong about the smell. Over time, it had grown less cloying, but it never entirely went away. Even after centuries, the house long crumbled, the subdivision turned, first, to waste, then to desert, then slowly, ever so slowly back to savanna, a traveler passing the spot where the bathroom once had been would note an unaccountable scent of calla lilies.

The End